William Shakespeare's 1 Henry VI, aka Henry VI, Part 1: A Retelling in Prose

David Bruce

Published by David Bruce, 2022.

This is a work of fiction. Similarities to real people, places, or events are entirely coincidental.

WILLIAM SHAKESPEARE'S 1 HENRY VI, AKA HENRY VI, PART 1: A RETELLING IN PROSE

First edition. July 26, 2022.

Copyright © 2022 David Bruce.

ISBN: 979-8201910914

Written by David Bruce.

Table of Contents

CAST OF CHARACTERS..1
CHAPTER 1 | — 1.1 —..4
— 1.2 —..11
— 1.3 —..17
— 1.4 —..22
— 1.5 —..26
— 1.6 —..28
CHAPTER 2 | — 2.1 —..30
— 2.2 —..34
— 2.3 —..36
— 2.4 —..39
— 2.5 —..45
CHAPTER 3 | — 3.1 —..49
— 3.2 —..57
— 3.3 —..63
— 3.4 —..66
CHAPTER 4 | — 4.1 —..68
— 4.2 —..75
— 4.3 —..77
— 4.4 —..79
— 4.5 —..81
— 4.6 —..83
— 4.7 —..85
CHAPTER 5 | — 5.1 —..89
— 5.2 —..91
— 5.3 —..92
— 5.4 —..100
— 5.5 —..106
Appendix A: Brief Historical Background 110
HOUSE OF LANCASTER..111
WARS OF THE ROSES 112
HOUSE OF YORK 113
A NOTE ON THE PLANTAGENETS..114

BEGINNING OF THE TUDOR DYNASTY 115
KING JAMES I OF ENGLAND: A MEMBER OF THE HOUSE OF STUART 117
A NOTE ON SHAKESPEARE 118
Appendix B: About the Author 119
Appendix C: Some Books by David Bruce 120

Dedication

DEDICATED TO MY SISTER MARTHA

Martha wrote, "When I was working at Longaberger, I worked with a girl who had two children and was in the middle of a divorce. She was so worried about Christmas for her boys. I received a very nice Christmas bonus that year, and I went to my boss and started a donation fund for the girl. My boss told me later that she — my boss —delivered the money to the girl's mother and father and told them not to tell her who brought the money for her. Months later the girl told me that the boys had the best Christmas that year, and she told me someone had brought money to her mom and dad for her, and she went to town and bought the boys Christmas. She never did know who did that for her. She was so thankful. I believe that I was the only one who donated to her, which was just fine."

***

The doing of good deeds is important. As a free person, you can choose to live your life as a good person or as a bad person. To be a good person, do good deeds. To be a bad person, do bad deeds. If you do good deeds, you will become good. If you do bad deeds, you will become bad. To become the person you want to be, act as if you already are that kind of person. Each of us chooses what kind of person we will become. To become a good person, do the things a good person does. To become a bad person, do the things a bad person does. The opportunity to take action to become the kind of person you want to be is yours.

Educate Yourself
Read Like A Wolf Eats
Be Excellent to Each Other
Books Then, Books Now, Books Forever

***

In this retelling, as in all my retellings, I have tried to make the work of literature accessible to modern readers who may lack the knowledge about mythology, religion, and history that the literary work's contemporary audience had.

Do you know a language other than English? If you do, I give you permission to translate this book, copyright your translation, publish or self-publish it, and keep all the royalties for yourself. (Do give me credit, of course, for the original retelling.)

I would like to see my retellings of classic literature used in schools, so I give permission to the country of Finland (and all other countries) to give copies of this book to all students forever. I also give permission to the state of Texas (and all other states) to give copies of this book to all students forever. I also give permission to all teachers to give copies of this book to all students forever.

Teachers need not actually teach my retellings. Teachers are welcome to give students copies of my eBooks as background material. For example, if they are teaching Homer's *Iliad* and *Odyssey*, teachers are welcome to give students copies of my *Virgil's* Aeneid: *A Retelling in Prose* and tell students, "Here's another ancient epic you may want to read in your spare time."

CAST OF CHARACTERS

English Male Characters

King Henry VI

Humphrey, Duke of Gloucester, uncle to the King, and Lord Protector. The Lord Protector, aka Protector of the Realm, is the individual ruler of England while the King is still a minor

Duke of Bedford, uncle to the King, and Regent of France. The Regent of France rules France while the King is still a minor

Thomas Beaufort, Duke of Exeter, great-uncle to the King

Henry Beaufort, great-uncle to the King, Bishop of Winchester, and afterwards Cardinal of Winchester

John Beaufort, Duke of Somerset

Richard Plantagenet, son of Richard, late Earl of Cambridge; afterwards Duke of York. In history, his children included King Edward IV and King Richard III

Earl of Warwick

Earl of Salisbury

Earl of Suffolk

Lord Talbot, afterwards Earl of Shrewsbury

John Talbot, his son

Edmund Mortimer, Earl of March

Sir John Fastolfe

Sir William Lucy

Sir William Glansdale

Sir Thomas Gargrave

Mayor of London

Woodville, Lieutenant of the Tower of London

Vernon, of the White-Rose, aka York faction

Basset, of the Red-Rose, aka Lancaster faction

A Lawyer

Mortimer's jail keepers

French Male Characters

Charles, Dauphin, and afterwards King of France. The Dauphin is the eldest son of the King of France; in this play/book, the person who is King of France is disputed

Reignier, Duke of Anjou, and titular King of Naples

Duke of Burgundy. Duke of Burgundy. His sister Anne married the Duke of Bedford, one of King Henry VI's uncles. King Henry VI refers to the Duke of Burgundy as an uncle

Duke of Alençon

Bastard of Orleans, aka Jean du Dunois, the illegitimate son of Louis I, the Duke of Orleans

Governor of Paris

Master Gunner of Orleans, and his Son

General of the French forces in Bordeaux

A French Sergeant

A Porter

An old Shepherd, father to Joan la Pucelle

Female Characters

Margaret, daughter to Reignier, afterwards married to King Henry VI

Countess of Auvergne, a Frenchwoman

Joan la Pucelle, commonly called Joan of Arc; "Pucelle" means "Maiden" or Virgin"; her father's name is Jacques d'Arc

Minor Characters

Lords, Warders of the Tower, Heralds, Officers, Soldiers, Messengers, and Attendants

Fiends appearing to Joan la Pucelle

Scene: England and France

Nota Bene:

King Henry V was born on 9 August 1386 and died on 31 August 1422.

King Henry VI (born 6 December 1421; died 21 May 1471) began his reign in 1422, but he was deposed on 1461; he briefly returned to the throne in 1470-1471.

The Hundred Years War, which lasted from 1337-1453 (116 years), was not fought continuously. The Edwardian War took place in 1337-1360; the Caroline War took place in 1369-1389; the Lancastrian War took place in 1415-1453.

After the Hundred Years War, the Wars of the Roses took place from 1455-1487. In those wars, the Yorkists and the Lancastrians fought for power in England. The emblem of the York family was a white rose, and the emblem of the Lancaster family was a red rose.

We read Shakespeare for drama, not history. He invents scenes and changes the ages of historical personages in his plays. He also changes the order in which historical events occur.

CHAPTER 1

— 1.1 —

King Henry V died on 31 August 1422. His son, who would become King Henry VI, was born on 6 December 1421. The Duke of Gloucester, young Henry's uncle, was named Protector of the Realm because of Henry's extreme youth.

The funeral of King Henry V was being held at Westminster Abbey. As funeral music played, pallbearers carried the coffin of the King. Present were the Duke of Bedford, who was also the Regent of France; the Duke of Gloucester, who was also the Lord Protector; the Duke of Exeter, the Earl of Warwick, the Bishop of Winchester, heralds, and attendants.

The Duke of Bedford said, "Let the Heavens be hung with black, and let day yield to night! Comets, predicting change of times and states, brandish your crystal-bright tresses in the sky, and with them scourge the bad mutinous stars that have consented to Henry's death!"

When a comet comes close to the Sun, it heats up and its gases form a tail. Because of that, comets were known in earlier ages as longhaired stars. The Greek word *kometes* means "longhaired."

He continued, "King Henry V was too famous to live long!"

A proverb stated, "Those whom God loves do not live long."

He continued, "England has never lost a King of so much worth."

The Duke of Gloucester said, "England never had a true King until the time of Henry V. Virtue, courage, and ability he had, and he deserved to command. His brandished sword blinded men with its reflected beams of Sunlight. His arms spread wider than a dragon's wings. His sparking eyes, replete with wrathful fire, dazzled and drove back his enemies more than the mid-day Sun fiercely turned against their faces. What should I say? His deeds exceed all speech; words fail me. He never lifted up his hand without conquering."

The Duke of Exeter said, "We mourn while wearing black. Why don't we mourn while covered in blood? Henry V is dead and never shall revive and come back to life. Upon a wooden coffin we attend, and Death's dishonorable victory we with our stately presence glorify, like captives bound to a triumphant chariot."

The ancient Romans held triumphal processions for conquering heroes. The conqueror would ride in a chariot with important captives bound and walking behind the chariot. In the Duke of Exeter's image, Death was the conqueror and the lords were the captives trailing behind Death's triumphal chariot.

He continued, "Shall we curse the planets of mishap — the planets that plotted thus our glory's overthrow?"

This society believed in astrology, which held that planets had an effect on Earth and its inhabitants. Some planets were malignant and could cause bad things — such as the death of King Henry V — to occur.

He continued, "Or shall we think the subtle-witted, cunning French are conjurers and sorcerers, who because they were afraid of him have contrived his end by the use of magic verses?"

This society also believed in magic that could be malignant and cause death. Since the English and the French were enemies, each side regarded the other side as employing conjurers and sorcerers.

The Bishop of Winchester said, "He was a King blessed by the King of Kings. The dreadful Judgment Day will not be as dreadful to the French as was the sight of him. The battles of the Lord of Hosts he fought; the church's prayers made him so prosperous."

Isaiah 13:4 states, "*The noise of a multitude in the mountains, like as of a great people; a tumultuous noise of the kingdoms of nations gathered together: the LORD of hosts mustereth the host of the battle*" (King James Version).

To "muster troops" means to "assemble troops." A "host" is an army.

"The church!" the Duke of Gloucester exclaimed. "Where is it? If churchmen had not prayed, his thread of life had not so soon decayed."

He believed that the churchmen had disliked King Henry V and had prayed for his death; he believed that they had preyed on him. He also was referring to the three Fates when he mentioned the thread of life. The three Fates spun the thread of life, measured it, and cut it. When an immortal Fate cut the thread of life, the mortal human died.

He continued, "You like none except an effeminate, weak, controllable Prince, whom, like a schoolboy, you may overawe."

All too often, people engage in power struggles. Many churchmen are not exempt from engaging in power politics. The reign of King Henry VI would be marked by many such political struggles, including this one between the Duke of Gloucester and the Bishop of Winchester.

The Bishop of Winchester replied, "Duke of Gloucester, whatever we like, you are the Lord Protector and you intend to command both the Prince and the realm. Your wife is proud; she makes you afraid of her more than God or religious churchmen can make you afraid."

"Don't talk about religion, for you love the flesh," the Duke of Gloucester said, "and never throughout the year do you go to church except to pray against your foes."

The Duke of Bedford said, "Stop! Stop these quarrels and rest your minds in peace. Let's go to the altar. Heralds, wait on us. Instead of gold, we'll offer up our weapons, since weapons are of no use to us now that King Henry V is dead. Posterity, expect wretched years, during which babes shall suck at their mothers' moist eyes, our isle shall be made a wet nurse of salt tears, and none but women shall be left to wail the dead.

"Henry V, your ghost I call upon. Make this realm prosper, keep it from civil broils, combat the malignant planets in the Heavens! A far more glorious star your soul will make than Julius Caesar or bright —"

After Julius Caesar's death, near the beginning of a festival held to celebrate him, a comet that was bright enough to be seen for seven days during daytime appeared. Many people believed that the comet was Julius Caesar's soul ascending into Heaven. (In this society, comets were sometimes called stars.)

A messenger entered Westminster Abbey and interrupted the Duke of Bedford: "My honorable lords, good health to you all! Sad tidings I bring to you from France, tidings of loss, of slaughters and utter defeat. The French cities of Guienne, Champagne, Rheims, Orleans, Paris, Guysors, and Poictiers are all quite lost."

"What are you saying, man, in front of dead King Henry V's corpse?" the Duke of Bedford asked. "Speak softly, or the loss of those great towns will make him burst out of his lead-lined coffin and rise from death."

"Is Paris lost? Has Rouen surrendered?" the Duke of Gloucester asked. "If Henry V were recalled to life again, this news would cause him once more to yield the ghost and die."

"How were they lost?" the Duke of Exeter asked. "What treachery was used?"

"No treachery," the messenger said, "but lack of men and money led to their loss. The soldiers mutter among themselves that here you maintain several factions, and while a field — an army and a battle — should be dispatched and fought, you are disputing about your Generals. One would have lingering wars with little cost. Another would fly swiftly, but lacks wings. A third thinks, with no expense at all, peace may be obtained by the use of guileful, pretty words.

"Awake, awake, English nobility! Don't let sloth dim your newly begotten honors — those French cities that King Henry V won for you! Cropped are the flower-de-luces in your arms; one half of England's coat of arms is cut away."

Flower-de-luces were French heraldic lilies; King Henry V and his son both had a claim to the French throne, and so one half of the coat of arms of the King of England displayed French lilies, the royal symbol of France.

The Duke of Exeter said, "If we lacked tears for this funeral, these tidings would call forth their flowing tides."

"These losses are my concern," the Duke of Bedford said. "I am the Regent of France: I rule there in the absence of the King of England. Give me my steeled coat of armor. I'll fight to regain France.

"Away with these disgraceful wailing robes! I will lend the French wounds, instead of eyes, to weep their intermittent miseries. Let their wounds cry bloody tears."

The miseries were intermittent because England and France fought intermittently. The Hundred Years War, which lasted from 1337-1453 (116 years), was not fought continuously. The Edwardian War took place in 1337-1360, the Caroline War took place in 1369-1389, and the Lancastrian War took place in 1415-1453.

After the Hundred Years War, the Wars of the Roses took place from 1455-1487.

Another messenger arrived and said, "Lords, view these letters full of bad mischance. Except for some petty towns of no importance, France has quite revolted from the English. Charles the Dauphin has been crowned King of Rheims. The Bastard of Orleans has joined with him. Reignier, Duke of Anjou, is on the Dauphin's side. The Duke of Alençon also flies to his side."

"The Dauphin has been crowned King of Rheims!" the Duke of Exeter exclaimed. "All fly to join him! Oh, where shall we fly from this disgrace?"

"We will not fly anywhere, except to our enemies' throats," the Duke of Gloucester said. "Duke of Bedford, if you are slack, I'll fight it out."

"Duke of Gloucester, why do you doubt my zeal to fight the French?" the Duke of Bedford asked. "I have mustered in my thoughts an army with which France is already overrun."

Another messenger arrived and said, "My gracious lords, to add to your laments, with which you now bedew with tears King Henry's hearse, I must inform you of a dismal fight between the brave, valiant Lord Talbot and the French."

The Bishop of Winchester said, "Talbot conquered the French, right?"

"Oh, no," the messenger replied. "In the battle Lord Talbot was defeated. I'll tell you the details at some length. On the tenth of August this dread-inspiring lord, retiring from the siege that we English were making of Orleans, having barely six thousand troops, was surrounded by twenty-three thousand French troops and set upon. He had no time to form his soldiers into battle formations. He lacked defensive ironbound pikes to set in the ground before his archers to protect them; instead, he used sharp stakes plucked out of hedges and set them in the ground confusedly and erratically to keep the enemy horsemen from breaking in and attacking the archers.

"The fight continued more than three hours, during which time valiant Talbot beyond what humans think possible enacted wonders with his sword and lance. Hundreds he sent to Hell, and none dared to face him. Here, there, and everywhere, he flew enraged. The French exclaimed that the Devil was fighting them. All the army stood and stared at him. His soldiers spying his undaunted spirit shouted forcefully the rallying cry 'To Talbot! To Talbot!' and rushed into the bowels — the midst — of the battle.

"Here the English would have fully defeated the French, if Sir John Fastolfe had not played the coward. He, placed just behind the front ranks with orders to relieve and follow them, instead cowardly fled, without having struck even one stroke.

"Henceforth grew the general destruction and massacre. Their enemies surrounded them. A base Belgium soldier, to win the French Dauphin's grace, thrust a spear into the back of Talbot, whom all the French soldiers with their finest assembled troops dared not look even once in the face."

"Has Talbot been slain?" the Duke of Bedford asked. "If he has, then I will slay myself for living idly here in pomp and ease while such a worthy leader, lacking aid, was betrayed to his despicable enemy."

"Oh, no, he lives," the messenger said, "but he was taken prisoner, along with Lord Scales and Lord Hungerford. Most of the rest were slaughtered or were also taken prisoner."

"His ransom none but I shall pay," the Duke of Bedford said. "I'll drag the Dauphin headlong from his throne. The Dauphin's crown shall be the ransom of my friend. Four of their lords I'll exchange for one of ours. For each English soldier killed, I'll four French soldiers.

"Farewell, my masters; to my task I go. I intend to make bonfires in France without delay in order to keep our great Saint George's feast that customarily follows great military victories. Ten thousand soldiers I will take with me, and their bloody deeds shall make all Europe quake with fear and awe."

The messenger said, "You need to do that. We are besieging the city of Orleans, which the French are holding. The English army has grown weak and faint. The Earl of Salisbury craves reinforcements and is hardly able to keep his men from mutinying since they, who are so few, look out over such a multitude of enemy soldiers."

"Remember, lords, your oaths you swore to King Henry V when he was on his deathbed," the Duke of Exeter said. "If the Dauphin rebelled, you swore either to utterly conquer him or to bring him in obedience to your yoke."

"I remember," the Duke of Bedford said, "and I here take my leave to go about my preparation for war."

He exited.

The Duke of Gloucester said, "I'll go to the Tower of London with all the haste I can to view the artillery and munitions, and then I will proclaim young Prince Henry our new King. He will be King Henry VI."

He exited.

The Duke of Exeter said, "I will go to Eltham, the royal residence, where the young King is. I have been appointed his special governor and am in charge of his education, and I'll make the best arrangements I can devise for his safety there."

He and everyone except the Bishop of Winchester exited.

Alone, the Bishop of Winchester said to himself, "Each of the other important persons has his place and function to attend, but I am left out; for me nothing remains. But not for long will I be Jack-out-of-office and have no influence on national and international affairs. I intend to steal the King from Eltham and sit at the chiefest stern of public weal. I intend to be the most important man in England."

Before the city of Orleans in France, Charles the Dauphin, the Duke of Alençon, and Reignier talked. Some soldiers, a drummer, and some attendants were present.

Charles the Dauphin said, "Mars' true moving, even as in the Heavens so in the Earth, to this day is not known."

This culture did not understand the motions of Mars the planet; to this culture, Mars seemed to move erratically in the night sky. Similarly, Mars the god of war seemed to erratically favor one side in a war and then the other side.

Charles the Dauphin continued, "Recently Mars shone and smiled on the English side. Now we are victors; upon us he smiles. We have all of the towns of any importance. At our pleasure we lie here near Orleans. Occasionally, the famished English, like pale ghosts, faintly and feebly besiege us one hour in a month."

The Duke of Alençon said, "The English lack their meat and vegetable stew and their fat bull-beef. Either they must be fed like mules and have their provender tied to their mouths in feed bags or else they will look piteous, like drowned mice."

Reignier said, "Let's raise the siege; let's put an end to it. Why do we live idly here? Talbot, whom we were accustomed to fear, has been captured. There remains no English military leader except the mad-brained Earl of Salisbury, and he may well spend his gall in fretting because he has neither men nor money to make war."

"Sound, sound the call to battle!" Charles the Dauphin said. "We will rush on them. Now for the honor of the forlorn French! I forgive any man who kills me when he sees me go back one foot or flee the battle."

The French and the English fought, and the English badly defeated the French.

"Who ever saw the like?" Charles the Dauphin said. "What 'men' I have! Dogs! Cowards! Dastards! I would never have fled except that they left me in the midst of my enemies."

Reignier said, "The Earl of Salisbury is a desperate homicide; he is a killer of men. He fights as if he were weary of his life. The other lords, like lions lacking food, rush hungrily upon us as if we were their prey."

The Duke of Alençon said, "Froissart, a 14th-century historian and countryman of ours, records that England bred only Olivers and Rowlands — great warriors — during the reign of King Edward III. More truly now this may be verified because England sends forth none but Samsons and Goliaths to skirmish with us. One Englishman to ten Frenchmen! The English are lean, raw-boned rascals! Who would ever suppose they had such courage and audacity?"

Literally, a rascal is a lean, inferior deer.

"Let's leave this town of Orleans," Charles the Dauphin said, "because the English are hare-brained slaves, and hunger will force them to be more fierce and eager to fight. Of old I know them; they would prefer to tear down the wall with their teeth rather than forsake the siege."

Reignier said, "I think that by some odd mechanical joints or device their arms are set like clocks so that they continually strike blows; otherwise, they could never hold out as they do. I agree that we should let them completely alone."

"Let it be so," the Duke of Alençon said.

The Bastard of Orleans arrived. He was the illegitimate son of Louis, the Duke of Orleans. He was also the nephew of King Charles VI, to whom Charles the Dauphin was the oldest surviving son.

The Bastard of Orleans said, "Where's the Prince Dauphin? I have news for him."

"Bastard of Orleans, you are thrice welcome to us," Charles the Dauphin said.

"I think your looks are sad and your face appalled and pale," the Bastard of Orleans said. "Has the recent defeat brought about this harm? Don't be dismayed, for succor is at hand. I have brought a holy virgin here with me; she is ordained by a vision sent to her from Heaven to raise this tedious siege and drive the English from the territory of France. The spirit of deep prophecy she has, exceeding the nine Sibyls — prophetesses — of old Rome. What's past and what's to come she can descry. Speak; shall I call her in? Believe my words, for they are certain and infallible."

"Go and call her in," Charles the Dauphin said.

The Bastard of Orleans exited.

Charles the Dauphin then said, "But first, to test her skill and knowledge, Reignier, you pretend to be me the Dauphin. Question her proudly and with dignity as a man of royalty would and let your looks be stern. By this means we shall find out what skill she has."

The Bastard of Orleans returned. With him was Joan la Pucelle — Joan the Virgin. History knows her as Joan of Arc.

Reignier asked, "Fair maiden, is it you who will do these wondrous feats?"

Joan la Pucelle replied, "Reignier, is it you who think to trick me? Where is the Dauphin?"

Seeing him behind some other people, she said, "Come, come out from behind them. I know thee well, though I have never seen thee before."

Joan la Pucelle's use of "thee" when talking to Charles the Dauphin was remarkable. "Thee" was used when talking to people of lower rank and when talking to friends and family and children. She did not lack confidence.

She continued, "Be not amazed, there's nothing hidden from me. In private I will talk with thee apart from the others.

"Stand back, you lords, and leave us alone awhile."

Reignier said, "She takes upon her bravely at first dash. She splendidly takes the initiative on first encountering the Dauphin."

Joan la Pucelle said, "Dauphin, I am by birth a shepherd's daughter, and my mind is untrained in any kind of art. Heaven and our gracious Lady — the Virgin Mary — have been pleased to shine on my contemptible state. While I took care of my tender lambs and displayed my cheeks to the Sun's parching heat, God's mother deigned to appear to me and in a vision full of majesty willed me to leave my base and lowborn vocation and free my country from calamity. She promised her aid and assured success. In complete glory she revealed herself, and although I was tanned and swarthy before, she used clear rays to infuse on me that beauty that I am blessed with and which you see. Ask me whatever questions you can possibly ask, and I will answer them unpremeditatedly. Test my courage by combat, if you dare, and you shall find that I surpass my sex. Be certain of this: You shall be fortunate if you accept me as your warlike companion."

Using the familiar "thou," Charles the Dauphin replied, "Thou has astonished me with your high terms and lofty utterance. Only this test I'll make of your valor: In single combat you shall buckle with me, and if you vanquish me, I will know your words are true, but if I vanquish you, I will renounce all confidence in you."

The word "buckle" meant "grapple." A bawdy-minded observer might think that the Dauphin and Joan grappling together might be a sexual "battle."

"I am prepared," Joan la Pucelle said. "Here is my keen-edged sword, decorated with five flower-de-luces on each side. I chose this sword at Touraine, in Saint Katharine's churchyard, out of a great deal of old iron."

"Then come and fight me, in God's name," Charles the Dauphin said. "I fear no woman."

"And while I live, I'll never flee from a man," Joan la Pucelle said.

A bawdy-minded observer might laugh after hearing this. Maidens sometimes fled from men to avoid being seduced or raped, but Joan would never flee from a man.

The two fought, and Joan la Pucelle defeated Charles the Dauphin.

"Stop! Stop fighting!" Charles the Dauphin pleaded. "You are an Amazon and you fight with the sword of Deborah."

The Amazons were mythological warrior women, and Deborah was a Jewish prophet, judge, and successful military commander; her story is told in Judges 4-5.

"Christ's mother helps me, else I would be too weak," Joan la Pucelle said.

"Whoever helps thee, it is you who must help me," Charles the Dauphin said. "Impatiently I burn with desire for thee. My heart and hands you have at once subdued. Excellent Pucelle, if that is your name, let me be your lover and not your sovereign. It is the French Dauphin who is saying this to thee."

"I must not yield to any rites of love, for my vow is consecrated from above," Joan la Pucelle said. "When I have chased all your foes from hence, then I will think about a recompense."

"In the meantime look gracious on your prostrate thrall," Charles the Dauphin said.

Joan la Pucelle was still sitting on him after vanquishing him, but in a moment they stood up.

"My lord, I think, is very long in talk," Reignier said. "They have been talking for a very long time."

"Doubtless he shrives this woman to her smock," the Duke of Alençon said. "Otherwise he could never protract his speech so long."

"To shrive" means "to hear confession"; a smock is a woman's undergarment. The Duke of Alençon was saying that Charles the Dauphin was hearing Joan la Pucelle's most intimate confessions.

"Shall we disturb him, since he keeps no mean?" Reignier asked. "He is observing no moderation, no mean between extremes."

"He may mean more than we poor men know," the Duke of Alençon said. "These women are shrewd tempters with their tongues."

"My lord, where are you?" Reignier asked. "What are you planning? Shall we give Orleans over to the enemy, or no?"

"Why, I say no, distrustful cowards!" Joan la Pucelle said, taking the enormous liberty of answering a question directed to Charles the Dauphin. "Fight until the last gasp; I will be your guardian."

"What she says I'll confirm," Charles the Dauphin said. "We'll fight it out."

"I am assigned to be the scourge of the English," Joan la Pucelle said. "This night I'll assuredly raise the siege and drive the English out of Orleans. Expect Saint Martin's summer, halcyon days, since I have entered into these wars."

She was saying to expect good times after the recent and current bad times. Saint Martin's Day is November 11, and good weather is especially welcome when it occurs in Europe on that date. The halcyon is a mythological bird identified with the kingfisher. This culture believed that the halcyon built nests on the sea, which remained calm until the nestlings were able to fly.

She continued, "Glory is like a circle in the water, a circle which never ceases to get bigger until by broad spreading it disperses to nothing. With King Henry V's death, the English circle ends; dispersed are the glories it included. Now I am like that proud insulting ship that bore Julius Caesar and his fortune at one and the same time."

Julius Caesar once needed to go to Brundisium, so in disguise he boarded a ship that encountered bad weather. The Captain of the ship was afraid, but Julius Caesar revealed his identity and told him not to be afraid because the ship carried both Caesar and Caesar's good fortune. Unfortunately for Joan's analogy, the ship was unable to complete the journey — it was forced to return, according to the Greek biographer Plutarch.

"Was Mahomet inspired by a dove?" Charles the Dauphin said. "If he was, then thou are inspired by an eagle."

A dove was said to thrust its beak into the prophet Muhammad's ear and reveal sacred knowledge to him. Non-believers thought that this was a trick, that Muhammad put crumbs of bread in his ear for the dove to eat.

This culture regarded the eagle as a nobler bird than the dove.

Charles the Dauphin continued, "Not even Saint Helena, the mother of great Constantine, nor yet Saint Philip's daughters, were like thee."

Saint Helena converted the Roman Emperor Constantine the Great to Christianity; in 313 C.E. he ordered that Christianity be tolerated rather than persecuted throughout the Roman Empire. A vision reputedly led Saint Helena to Calgary, where she discovered the cross on which Christ had been crucified.

Saint Philip's daughters were prophets. According to Acts 21:9, "*And the same man had four daughters, virgins, which did prophesy*" (King James Version).

Charles the Dauphin continued, "Bright star of Venus, fallen down on the Earth, how may I reverently worship thee enough?"

This was ominous. God ought to be worshipped, not Joan la Pucelle. Also, Venus is a pagan goddess, not connected with Christianity the way that Saint Helena and Saint Philip's daughters are. Furthermore, Venus is both the evening star and the morning star. Lucifer is the name given to Satan before he fell to Earth and into Hell — thought by this culture to be located at the center of the Earth — after rebelling against God in Heaven; "Lucifer" means "morning star."

"Leave off delays, and let us raise the siege," the Duke of Alençon said. "Let's get started."

"Woman, do what you can to save our honors," Reignier said. "Drive the English from Orleans, and be immortalized."

Apparently, Reignier thought less of Joan la Pucelle than Charles the Dauphin did, since he called her "Woman" rather than "Bright star of Venus."

"We'll try immediately to raise the siege," Charles the Dauphin said. "Come, let's go and get started. I will trust no prophet, if Joan la Pucelle proves to be a false prophet."

In London, before the Tower of London, the Duke of Gloucester stood. With him were some serving men, dressed in blue coats; blue was the color traditionally worn by serving men. The Tower of London was a fortress, a prison, and the main armory of London.

The Duke of Gloucester said, "I have come to survey the Tower of London this day. Since King Henry V's death, I fear, weapons have been stolen from the armory. Where are the guards who ought to be here? Open the gates. It is the Duke of Gloucester who is calling to be admitted."

The first guard said from inside, "Who's out there who knocks so imperiously?"

The first serving man replied, "It is the noble Duke of Gloucester."

The second guard said, "Whoever he is, you may not be let in."

The first serving man replied, "Villains, do you answer that way to the Duke of Gloucester, who is the Lord Protector?"

The first guard said, "May the Lord protect him! That is how we answer him. We do no otherwise than we are ordered to do."

"Who ordered you to keep me out?" the Duke of Gloucester asked. "Whose orders ought you to take but mine? There's no Protector of the Realm other than me."

He ordered his serving men, "Break up the gates; I'll be your warranty. Shall I be flouted thus by dunghill grooms?"

Dunghill grooms were servants who cleared away the dung left by horses and other animals.

The Duke of Gloucester's serving men rushed at the Tower Gates.

Lieutenant Woodville spoke from inside the Tower of London, "What noise is this? What traitors have we here?"

The Duke of Gloucester said, "Lieutenant Woodville, is it your voice I hear? Open the gates. I am the Duke of Gloucester, and I want to enter."

"Be calm, noble Duke," Lieutenant Woodville said. "I may not open the gates. The Cardinal of Winchester forbids me to do so. From him I have the explicit command that neither you nor any of your servants shall be let in."

"Faint-hearted Woodville, do you value him more than you value me? Do you value the arrogant Bishop of Winchester, that haughty prelate, whom Henry V, our late sovereign, never could endure?"

Henry Beaufort was the Bishop of Winchester. The Pope had made him also the Cardinal of Winchester, but the late King Henry V had refused to allow him to be installed as Cardinal. Now that Henry V was dead, the Bishop of Winchester was wearing the red clothing of a Cardinal, although he would not wear it while at court — yet. Later, King Henry VI would allow him to be installed as Cardinal of Winchester and so he would be addressed that way by everyone and he would wear the red robes of a Cardinal openly.

The Bishop of Winchester and the Duke of Gloucester were related. The Duke of Gloucester's father was King Henry IV. The Bishop of Winchester was King Henry IV's half-brother. When the Bishop of Winchester was born, his parents were not married, but they married afterward. John of Gaunt is the Bishop of Winchester's father and the Duke of Gloucester's grandfather.

The Duke of Gloucester said to Lieutenant Woodville, using "thou," which was used when speaking to men of inferior social status, "Thou are no friend to God or to the King. Open the gates, or I'll shut thee out shortly."

"Shut thee out" may have meant to shut him out of the Tower of London or to remove him from his job, or both.

The Duke of Gloucester's serving men said, "Open the gates for the Lord Protector, or we'll burst them open, if you don't quickly obey."

The Bishop of Gloucester arrived at the Tower gates. Accompanying him were his attendants, who wore tawny clothing.

"Greetings, ambitious Humphrey!" the Bishop of Winchester said to the Duke of Gloucester, whose given name was Humphrey. "What does all this commotion mean?"

"Peeled priest, do you command me to be shut out of the Tower of London?" the Duke of Gloucester asked.

A peeled priest was a tonsured priest. A priest of the time would shave the top of his head.

"Peeled" sounded like "pilled," which meant "threadbare." Priests were supposed to be humble, but the Bishop of Winchester was wearing the magnificent red robes of a Cardinal.

The Bishop of Winchester replied, "I command you to be shut out of the Tower of London, you most usurping proditor, and not Protector, of the King and realm."

"Proditor" is an unusual word that means "traitor."

The Duke of Gloucester said, "Stand back, you manifest conspirator, thou who contrived to murder our dead lord, King Henry V, when he was an infant — thou who gives whores indulgences to sin. I'll toss thee in your broad Cardinal's hat as if it were a canvas sheet if you proceed in this insolence of yours."

The Bishop of Winchester was known for having land on which brothels stood, and so part of his income came from madams and pimps. An indulgence was a sheet of paper that supposedly gave forgiveness of sin in return for a good deed, which usually consisted of a donation to the Catholic Church.

The Bishop of Winchester replied, "No, you stand back. I will not budge a foot. This can be Damascus, and you can be cursed Cain here to slay Abel, your brother, if you want."

In this culture, people believed that the city of Damascus was built on the location where Cain murdered Abel, his brother.

"I will not slay thee, but I'll drive thee back," the Duke of Gloucester said. "Thy scarlet robes as a child's bearing-cloth I'll use to carry thee out of this place."

A bearing-cloth was a christening cloth. The baby was carried in it to the location where it would be baptized.

"Do whatever you dare to do," the Bishop of Winchester said. "I beard thee to your face."

"To beard someone" meant "to grab his beard and pull it" — this was a calculated and major insult.

"What!" the Duke of Gloucester said. "Am I dared and bearded to my face? Draw your swords, men, despite this being a privileged place."

Some places, such as the Tower of London and royal residences, were privileged. Drawn swords and violence were forbidden in those places.

He continued, "Blue coats against tawny coats. Priest, look after your beard because I mean to tug it and to beat you soundly."

He then stamped his feet and said, "Under my feet I stamp your Cardinal's hat in spite of Pope or dignities of church. Here I'll drag thee up and down by your bearded cheeks."

"Duke of Gloucester, you will answer for this before the Pope," the Bishop of Winchester said.

"Winchester goose, I cry, 'A rope! A rope!'" the Duke of Gloucester said.

A Winchester goose was a swelling in the groin that was caused by venereal disease; it also meant a prostitute in the area where the Bishop of Winchester owned much land. Parrots were taught to cry "A rope! A rope!" as a kind of joke. The parrot was supposedly calling for a rope to be used to hang someone.

The Duke of Gloucester ordered his serving men, "Now beat them away from here. Why do you let them stay?"

He then said to the Bishop of Winchester, "Thee I'll chase away from here, you wolf in sheep's clothing.

"Get out, tawny coats! Get out, scarlet hypocrite!"

The two groups of men fought, and the Duke of Gloucester's men beat back the Bishop of Winchester's men. While the fighting was going on, the Mayor of London and his officers arrived.

"Bah, lords!" the Mayor of London shouted, "It's a disgrace that you, who are supreme magistrates, thus contumeliously — disgracefully and contemptuously — should break the peace!"

"Be calm, Mayor!" the Duke of Gloucester said. "You know little about my wrongs: Here's Beaufort, the Bishop of Winchester, who respects neither God nor King; he has here seized the Tower of London for his own use."

The Bishop of Winchester said to the Mayor, "Here's the Duke of Gloucester, a foe to citizens, a man who always proposes war and never peace, who overcharges your generous purses with large taxes and levies, who seeks to overthrow religion because he is Protector of the Realm, and who would take the armor here out of the Tower of London and use it to crown himself King and suppress the Prince who is supposed to be crowned King Henry VI."

"I will not answer thee with words, but with blows," the Duke of Gloucester said.

He hit the Bishop of Winchester.

"Nothing remains to be done by me in this tumultuous strife but to make open proclamation," the Mayor said.

He ordered, "Come, officer; as loudly as you can, cry out the open proclamation."

As the officer knew, part of the Mayor's duty was to keep the peace.

The officer shouted, "All manner of men assembled here in arms this day against God's peace and the King's, we charge and command you, in his highness' name, to go to your separate dwelling places, and we charge and command you not to wear, handle, or use any sword, weapon, or dagger, henceforward, upon pain of death."

"Cardinal, I'll be no breaker of the law," the Duke of Gloucester said to the Bishop of Winchester. He used the word "Cardinal" as a gesture to show the Mayor that he would keep the peace.

He added, "But we shall meet, and break our minds at large. We will have words and thoroughly let each other know what we think."

The Bishop of Winchester replied, "Duke of Gloucester, we will meet — to your cost, you can be sure. I will have thy heart's blood for this day's work."

"I'll call for clubs, if you will not go away," the Mayor said.

If he were to have the officer call for clubs, the city's apprentices would come running, carrying clubs that they would use to separate two groups who were fighting.

The Mayor then said to himself, "This Cardinal's more haughty than the Devil."

"Mayor, farewell," the Duke of Gloucester said. "You are only doing your job."

"Abominable Gloucester, guard your head," the Bishop of Winchester said, "because I intend to have it before long."

The Duke of Gloucester and the Bishop of Winchester exited in two separate directions, along with all their men.

The Mayor ordered, "See that the coast is cleared, and then we will depart."

He then said to himself, "Good God, I can't believe that these nobles should bear such anger! I myself have fought not even once in forty years."

— 1.4 —

A French Master Gunner and his son stood on the wall of Orleans beside a cannon.

The Master Gunner said to his son, "Sirrah, you know how Orleans is besieged by the English, and how the English have won the suburbs surrounding the city."

Fathers called their sons "sirrah," a form of address that people of high status used to address males of lower status.

"Father, I know," the boy said, "and I often have shot at them; however, unfortunately I have always missed my target."

The Master Gunner said, "But now you shall not miss."

He meant that the boy would not now fire the cannon; however, the boy, as will be seen, would disobey that order.

The Master Gunner continued, "Do what I tell you to do. I am the Chief Master Gunner of this town, and I must do something that will bring me honor. The ruler's spies have informed me that the English, who are closely entrenched in the suburbs, are accustomed, through a secret grate of iron bars in yonder tower, to look out over the city, and from there discover how with most advantage they may vex us with shot, or with assault."

The English had captured a high tower that had been built at the end of a bridge crossing the Loire River. The Master Gunner and his son were in the high tower at the end of the bridge closest to Orleans.

The Master Gunner continued, "To prevent this inconvenience, I have placed opposing that tower this piece of ordnance, and for the past three days I have watched to see if the English lords would appear there. Now I want you to watch because I can stay here no longer. If you see any English lords, run and bring the information to me; you shall find me at the governor's."

"Don't worry, father," the boy said.

The Master Gunner exited.

His son said to himself, "Father, I promise you that you don't need to worry that I will bother you with any news. I'll never trouble you, if I may see any English lords."

He meant that he would fire the cannon and get the glory for himself.

On the tower, some English lords now arrived: the Earl of Salisbury, as well as Lord Talbot, Sir Thomas Gargrave, and Sir William Glansdale, and others. From the tower, they were able to look down on Orleans and plan where to attack next. But first they talked together and got news from Lord Talbot, who had recently been a prisoner.

The Earl of Salisbury said, "Lord Talbot, my life, my joy, returned again to us! How were you treated when you were prisoner? By what means were you released? Tell us, please, while we are here on this tower's top."

Lord Talbot replied, "The Duke of Bedford had a prisoner called the brave Lord Ponton de Santrailles. I was exchanged and ransomed for him. But to show contempt for me, my captors would once have bartered me for a baser man of arms by far. This I, disdaining, scorned. I craved death rather than be so vilely esteemed as to be exchanged for such a base, lowly born man. To conclude, I was redeemed as I desired.

"But the treacherous Fastolfe wounds my heart. I would execute and kill him with my bare fists, if I now had him brought within my power."

The Earl of Salisbury said, "You haven't yet said how you were treated when you were a prisoner."

Lord Talbot replied, "I was treated with scoffs and scorns and contumelious taunts. They displayed me in the open marketplace and made me a public spectacle to all. Here, they said, is the terror of the French, the scarecrow that frightens our children so. Then I broke away from the officers who led me, and I dug with my fingernails stones out of the ground to hurl at the beholders of my shame. My menacing countenance made others flee. None dared come near me for fear of sudden death.

"Even within iron walls they deemed me not safely secured. Such great fear of my name had spread among them that they supposed I could break bars of steel, and kick into pieces posts made of the hardest material. Therefore I had as guards their best marksmen, who walked around me at intervals, and if I only moved out of my bed, they were ready to shoot me in the heart."

The Master Gunner's son lit a gunner's match and placed it in a linstock, a piece of wood with a fork at one end into which the match was placed. That way, the cannon could be fired from a short, but safer, distance.

The Earl of Salisbury said, "I grieve to hear what torments you endured, but we will be revenged sufficiently. Now it is suppertime in Orleans. Here, through this grate, I can count each Frenchman and view how the Frenchmen fortify the city. Let us look at the city; the sight will much delight you.

"Sir Thomas Gargrave, and Sir William Glansdale, let me have your carefully considered opinions about the best place to make our next attack."

Sir Thomas Gargrave said, "I think we should make our attack at the north gate because lords are standing there."

Sir William Glansdale said, "And I think we should make our attack here, at the bulwark of the bridge."

Lord Talbot said, "From what I can see, we must starve the citizens of this city as a military strategy, or weaken it with light skirmishes."

The Master Gunner's son shot the cannon.

The Earl of Salisbury and Sir Thomas Gargrave both fell, mortally wounded.

The Earl of Salisbury said, "Oh, Lord, have mercy on us wretched sinners!"

Sir Thomas Gargrave said, "Oh, Lord, have mercy on me, a woeful man!"

"What mischance is this that has suddenly crossed us?" Lord Talbot said. "Speak, Earl of Salisbury; at least, if you can speak, tell us how you are, you mirror and paragon of all martial men? One of your eyes and your cheek's side have been struck off! Accursed tower! Accursed fatal hand that has contrived this woeful tragedy!

"The Earl of Salisbury conquered in thirteen battles. He was the first who trained King Henry V in warfare. While any trumpeter sounded, or any drummer struck, his sword never stopped striking in the battlefield.

"Are you still living, Earl of Salisbury? Though your speech fails, you still have one eye to look to Heaven for grace and mercy. The Sun with its one eye views the entire world.

"Heaven, be gracious to no one who is alive, if the Earl of Salisbury lacks mercy at your hands!

"Sir Thomas Gargrave, do you have any life left? Speak to me, or look up at me."

Sir Thomas Gargrave was dead.

Lord Talbot ordered, "Carry his body away; I will help to bury it."

He then said, "Earl of Salisbury, cheer your spirit with this comfort. You shall not die while —."

He did not finish his sentence, but instead said about the Earl of Salisbury, "He beckons with his hand and smiles at me like a man who would say, 'When I am dead and gone, remember to avenge me on the French.' Plantagenet, I will."

The Earl of Salisbury's family name was not Plantagenet, but he was related to the Plantagenets.

Lord Talbot continued, "And I will, like you, Roman Emperor Nero, play on the lute as I watch the towns burn. Wretched and fearful shall the French be if they only hear my name."

The Roman Emperor Nero was said to have played music while watching Rome burn.

A battle call sounded, and lightning flashed and thunder rumbled.

Lord Talbot asked, "What commotion is this? What tumult is in the Heavens? From where comes this call to battle and this noise?"

A messenger arrived and said, "My lord, my lord, the French have gathered a fighting force. The Dauphin, who has joined with one Joan la Pucelle, a newly risen holy prophetess, has come with a great army to raise the siege."

The Earl of Salisbury raised himself up on one arm and groaned.

Lord Talbot said, "Hear, hear how the dying Salisbury groans! It irks his heart that he cannot be revenged. Frenchmen, I'll be a Salisbury to you. Pucelle or puzel, dolphin or dogfish, your hearts I'll stamp out with my horse's heels, and I'll make a quagmire of your mingled brains."

A "puzel" was a whore. The dolphin was a highly regarded creature of the sea, while a dogfish — a species of small shark — was a lowly regarded creature of the sea.

Lord Talbot ordered, "Convey the Earl of Salisbury for me into his tent, and then we'll try what these dastardly Frenchmen dare. We will fight these cowardly French soldiers."

The battle began. Lord Talbot fought Charles the Dauphin and drove him back. Joan la Pucelle fought some English soldiers and drove them back.

Lord Talbot said to himself, "Where is my strength, my valor, and my force? Our English troops retreat, and I cannot stop them. A woman clad in armor chases them."

Joan la Pucelle approached him.

Lord Talbot said to himself, "Here, here she comes."

He then said to Joan la Pucelle, "I'll have a bout with thee. Devil or devil's dam, I'll conjure thee. Blood will I draw on thee, for you are a witch, and without delay I will give your soul to him — the Devil — whom you serve."

People in this culture believed that if you drew blood from a witch, you could gain control over her.

"Come, come," Joan la Pucelle said. "It is only I who must disgrace thee."

They fought.

"Heavens, can you suffer Hell so to prevail?" Lord Talbot said in a brief break from fighting. "My breast I'll burst with the straining of my courage and I'll crack my arms asunder, but I *will* chastise this high-minded strumpet."

They fought again.

"Talbot, farewell," Joan la Pucelle said. "Your hour to die has not yet come. I must go and provide Orleans with provisions immediately."

She and her soldiers prepared to go into the town.

She then said to Lord Talbot, "Attack me, if you can; I scorn your strength. Go, go, cheer up your famished men who are dying of hunger. Help the Earl of Salisbury to make his testament. This day is ours, as many more shall be."

She and the French soldiers exited.

Lord Talbot said to himself, "My thoughts are whirled like a potter's wheel. I don't know where I am, nor what I am doing. A witch, using fear, not force, like Hannibal, drives back our troops and conquers as she wishes. Similarly, bees with smoke and doves with noisome stench are driven away from their hives and houses. The French called us for our fierceness English dogs. Now, like puppies, we run away, crying."

Hannibal was a Carthaginian General who crossed the Alps and entered Roman territory, where he terrorized the Romans while roaming up and down the Roman territory at will.

A military trumpet sounded.

Lord Talbot said, "Hark, countrymen! Either renew the fight, or tear the lions out of England's coat. Renounce your soil, give sheep in lions' stead: Sheep run not half as treacherously from the wolf, or horse or oxen from the leopard, as you fly from your often-subdued slaves."

To flee the enemy can be treacherous. Not only is the battle lost, but great loss of life can occur during an unorganized retreat. Lord Talbot was saying that the English soldiers needed to regroup and fight well, or they might as well replace the lions in the English flag with sheep.

A military trumpet sounded and a short fight took place.

Lord Talbot said, "A victory for us will not be. Retire into your trenches. You all consented to the Earl of Salisbury's death, for none of you would strike a stroke with your swords in his revenge. Joan la Pucelle has entered Orleans, in spite of us or anything that we could do. I wish that I would die with the Earl of Salisbury! The shame of his death will make me hide my head."

On the wall of Orleans stood Joan la Pucelle, Charles the Dauphin, Reignier, the Duke of Alençon, and some soldiers.

Joan la Pucelle said, "Advance our waving battle flags on the wall; we have rescued Orleans from the English. Thus Joan la Pucelle has performed what she gave her word she would do."

Charles the Dauphin said to her, "Divinest creature, Astraea's daughter, how shall I honor thee for this success?"

Astraea is a mythological Greek goddess of justice. When she left Earth, the Iron Age began. When she returns to Earth, a new Golden Age will begin.

He continued, "Thy promises are like Adonis' gardens that bloomed one day and gave fruit the next day."

Adonis was a figure in various ancient Greek mystery religions; the plants in his garden grew quickly.

Charles the Dauphin then said, "France, triumph in your glorious prophetess! The town of Orleans has been recovered. A more blessed event never befell our state."

Reignier said, "Why not order the bells to be rung aloud throughout the town? Dauphin, command the citizens to make bonfires and feast and banquet in the open streets to celebrate the joy that God has given us."

The Duke of Alençon said, "All France will be replete and satisfied with mirth and joy when they shall hear how we have played the roles of men and fought bravely."

"It is by Joan, not we, that the day is won," Charles the Dauphin said. "Because of this victory, I will divide my crown with her, and all the priests and friars in my realm shall in procession sing her endless praise. A statelier pyramid to her I'll rear than Rhodope's pyramid at Memphis ever was."

Rhodope was a 6th-century B.C.E. Greek courtesan who became very wealthy from her profession and was said to have built a pyramid at Memphis, Egypt. She was also said to have eventually married the King of Egypt.

Charles the Dauphin continued, "In memory of her when she is dead, her ashes, in an urn more precious than the richly jeweled coffer of Darius, shall be transported at high festivals before the Kings and Queens of France."

When Alexander the Great conquered the city of Gaza, among the spoils was a richly jeweled coffer that had belonged to the Persian King Darius, who had unsuccessfully tried to conquer Greece but was defeated in 490 B.C.E. in the Battle of Marathon. Alexander used the coffer to carry his most precious possession: the epic poems of Homer.

Charles the Dauphin continued, "No longer on Saint Denis, the patron saint of France, will we cry, but Joan la Pucelle shall be France's saint. Come in, and let us banquet royally, after this golden day of victory."

CHAPTER 2

— 2.1 —

On the wall protecting Orleans, which was now controlled by the French, a Sergeant gave orders to two sentinels who would guard the city: "Sirs, take your places and be vigilant. If you hear any noise or see any enemy soldier near the wall, by some evident sign let us have knowledge at the guardhouse."

"Sergeant, you shall," the first sentinel said.

The Sergeant exited.

The first sentinel said, "Thus are poor servitors — common soldiers — compelled to watch in darkness, rain, and cold, while others sleep upon their quiet beds."

Lord Talbot, the Duke of Bedford, the Duke of Burgundy, and some soldiers arrived. They were carrying scaling ladders. A drummer beat quietly on a muffled drum as the soldiers marched. The Duke of Bedford was the Regent of France; he ruled France in King Henry VI's stead. The Duke of Burgundy was French, but he sided with England.

Lord Talbot said, "Lord Regent, and feared Duke of Burgundy, by whose arrival the regions of Artois, Wallon, and Picardy are now friends to us, this fortunate night the Frenchmen are unsuspecting and overconfident after having all day caroused and banqueted. We therefore embrace this opportunity as being best fit to repay their deceit contrived by magical art and baleful sorcery. They defeated us with witchcraft."

"Coward of France!" the Duke of Bedford said, referring to the Dauphin of France. "How much he dishonors his fame and reputation by despairing of his own arm's fortitude and joining with witches and using the help of Hell!"

The Duke of Burgundy said, "Traitors never have other company, but who's that Pucelle whom they term so pure?"

"She is a maiden — a virgin — they said," Lord Talbot replied.

"A maiden!" the Duke of Bedford said. "And yet she is so martial!"

The Duke of Burgundy said, "Pray to God that she proves not to be masculine before long, if underneath the standard of the French she continues to carry armor as she has begun."

The Duke of Burgundy felt that if Joan were to turn out to be a man under her armor, then things would go even worse for the English; therefore, he wanted the Duke of Bedford to pray to God that Joan really was a woman. One way for her to be proven to be female would be for her to become pregnant.

His words contained wordplay. The "standard of the French" could be a French battle flag or a French penis, since a standard is a thing that can stand up. For Joan to carry armor could mean for her to wear armor or for her to bear, aka carry, the weight — during sex — of a man, such as the Dauphin, who wears armor.

Lord Talbot said, "Well, let them practice and converse with spirits."

His words also contained wordplay. In this culture, the words "practice" and "converse" both had the meaning of "have sex with."

He continued, "God is our fortress, and in His conquering name let us resolve to scale the flinty bulwarks of the French."

"Ascend, brave Talbot," the Duke of Bedford said, "We will follow you."

"Let's not all climb up the same scaling ladder together," Lord Talbot said. "It's far better, I guess, that we make our entrance in several places, so that if it happens that one of us fails, then the others may rise against the French force."

"I agree," the Duke of Bedford said. "I'll go to yonder corner."

"And I will go to this corner," the Duke of Burgundy said.

Lord Talbot said, "And here will I, Talbot, mount and climb high, or make my grave. Now, Earl of Salisbury, for you, and for the right of English Henry VI, shall this night show how much in duty I am bound to both. I am doing this for both the Earl of Salisbury and King Henry VI."

They started the attack, and the French sentinels cried, "Arm yourselves! Arm yourselves! The enemy is making an assault on us! The English are attacking us!"

The English soldiers attacked while shouting out such rallying cries as "St. George" and "To Talbot!"

The French were surprised, and some leaped over the wall in their night clothing.

The Bastard of Orleans, the Duke of Alençon, and Reignier, all of whom were in disarray and wearing only part of their armor, which they had hastily put on, appeared.

The Duke of Alençon said, "How are all of you now, my lords! Are all of us so unready to fight back?"

"Unready!" the Bastard of Orleans exclaimed. "Yes, we are, and we are glad we escaped so well. At least we are still alive."

Reignier said, "It was time, I thought, for us to wake up and leave our beds since we were hearing battle calls outside our chamber doors."

The Duke of Alençon said, "Of all exploits since I first followed arms, I have never heard of a warlike enterprise more adventurous or risky than this."

The Bastard of Orleans said, "I think this Talbot is a fiend of Hell."

Reignier said, "If he is not a creature of Hell, then the Heavens surely favor him."

"Here comes Charles the Dauphin," the Duke of Alençon said, looking up. "I wonder how he sped. I wonder how he got on during the attack."

The Bastard of Orleans said, "Tut, holy Joan was his defensive guard."

He may have meant that Joan la Pucelle was in bed with Charles the Dauphin when the attack started. If so, "holy Joan" meant "Joan, who has a hole."

Charles the Dauphin and Joan la Pucelle went over to them.

Charles the Dauphin said to Joan la Pucelle, "Is this your cunning, you deceitful dame? Did you at first, to flatter us, make us partakers of a little gain, so that now our loss might be ten times as much?"

"Why is Charles the Dauphin impatient with his friend?" Joan la Pucelle said. "Do you think that my power is at all times alike? Must I always prevail whether I am asleep or awake, and if I do not will you blame me and lay the fault on me?

"Improvident soldiers! If your watch had been good, this sudden evil misfortune never could have happened."

Charles the Dauphin said, "Duke of Alençon, this was your fault because as Captain of the watch this night, you took no better care for that weighty responsibility."

The Duke of Alençon said to the others, "Had all your quarters been as safely kept as that whereof I had the command, we would not have been thus shamefully surprised."

"The part under my command was secure," the Bastard of Orleans said.

"And so was mine, my lord," Reignier said.

Charles the Dauphin said, "And, as for myself, for the most part of all this night, within Joan la Pucelle's quarters and my own precinct I was employed in passing to and fro and in relieving the sentinels. Therefore how or in which way did the English first break in?"

Joan la Pucelle said, "Discuss, my lords, no further about the case, how or in which way this misfortune happened. It is certain that they found some place only weakly guarded, and that is where the breach was made. And now there remains nothing to do but this: We must gather our soldiers, who are scattered and dispersed, and form new plans to damage the English army."

A military trumpet sounded, and an English soldier ran onto the scene, crying "To Talbot! To Talbot!" The French fled, leaving behind pieces of armor and weapons they had been carrying.

The English soldier said, "I'll be so bold as to take what they have left behind. The cry of 'To Talbot!' serves me like a sword for I have loaded myself with many spoils, using no other weapon but his name."

— 2.2 —

The English had taken the town of Orleans. Inside the town, Lord Talbot, the Duke of Bedford, the Duke of Burgundy, a Captain, and some others were standing.

The Duke of Bedford said, "The day begins to break, and it now has fled the night, whose pitch-black mantle over-veiled the Earth. Here we will sound retreat and cease our hot pursuit."

The retreat sounded.

Lord Talbot said, "Bring forth the body of the old Earl of Salisbury, and here raise it in the marketplace, the middle center of this cursed town. Now I have paid the vow I made to his soul; for every drop of blood that was drawn from him, at least five Frenchmen have died tonight. And so that future ages may behold what devastation happened in revenge of him, within their most important temple — the cathedral — I'll erect a tomb in which his corpse shall be interred. Upon the tomb so that everyone may read it shall be engraved the sack of Orleans, the treacherous manner of his mournful death, and what a terror he had been to France.

"But, lords, in all our bloody massacre, I wonder that we did not meet with his 'grace' the Dauphin, his newly come champion — the 'virtuous' Joan of Arc — or with any of his false confederates."

The Duke of Bedford said, "It is thought, Lord Talbot, that when the fight began, roused suddenly from their drowsy beds, amongst the troops of armed men they leapt over the wall in order to find refuge in the fields."

The Duke of Burgundy said, "As for myself, as far as I could well see through the smoke and dusky vapors of the night, I am sure I scared the Dauphin and his slut; they both came swiftly running arm in arm as if they were a pair of loving turtledoves that could not live apart day or night. After things are set in order here, we'll follow them with all the power we have."

A messenger arrived and said, "All hail, my lords! Which of this Princely train do you call the warlike Talbot because of his acts throughout the realm of France that are so much applauded?"

Lord Talbot said, "Here is the Talbot. Who wants to speak with him?"

The messenger replied, "The virtuous French lady, the Countess of Auvergne, with modesty admiring your renown, by me entreats, great lord, you to agree to visit her poor castle where she lives, so that she may boast she has beheld the man whose glory fills the world with loud acclamation."

The Duke of Burgundy said, "Is that so? So, then, I see that our wars will turn into a peaceful comic sport, when ladies crave to be encountered with."

One meaning of "to encounter" was "to have sex."

He added, "You may not, my lord, despise her gentle request. You must see her."

"Never trust me if I despise her gentle request," Lord Talbot said, "for when a world of men could not prevail with all their oratory and rhetoric, yet a woman's kindness has prevailed, and therefore, messenger, tell her that I return great thanks to her and as she requests I will visit her."

He then asked the other lords, "Will not your honors bear me company when I visit her?"

"No, truly," the Duke of Bedford said. "It is more than manners demand, and I have heard it said that uninvited guests are often most welcome when they are gone."

"Well then I will go alone, since there's no remedy," Lord Talbot said. "I mean to try this lady's courtesy."

He then said, "Come here, Captain."

He whispered to the Captain and then asked, "Do you understand your orders?"

The Captain replied, "I do, my lord, and I will obey them."

The Countess of Auvergne and her porter were in her castle, preparing for Lord Talbot's visit. Porters take care of gates and entrances.

She said, "Porter, remember what I ordered you to do, and when you have done that, bring the keys to me."

"Madam, I will," the porter said, and then he exited.

Alone, the Countess of Auvergne said to herself, "The plot is laid. If all things fall out right, as a result of this exploit I shall become as famous as the Scythian Tomyris became by Cyrus the Great's death."

Tomyris, the Queen of the Scythians, sought revenge for the death of her son, who committed suicide after being captured by the Persian King Cyrus the Great's army. Queen Tomyris led an army against Cyrus the Great's army, and her army was triumphant and killed Cyrus the Great. According to the Greek historian Herodotus, she had Cyrus the Great's body decapitated and then took his head and shoved it into a wineskin filled with human blood, saying as she did so, "I warned you that I would quench your thirst for blood!"

The Countess of Auvergne continued, "Great is the rumored reputation of this dreaded knight, and his achievements are of no less account. My eyes and my ears would gladly witness him so that they can criticize and judge these rare reports."

The messenger entered the room, accompanied by Lord Talbot, who was carrying a horn.

The messenger said, "Madam, just as your ladyship desired, and by message craved, so has Lord Talbot come to visit you."

"And he is welcome," the Countess of Auvergne said. "What! Is this the man?"

"Madam, he is," the messenger said.

"Is this man the scourge of France?" the Countess of Auvergne asked. "Is this the Talbot, who is so much feared abroad that with his name mothers quiet their babes? I see that the reports about him are fabulous and false. I thought that I should have seen some Hercules, a second Hector, for his grim aspect, and the large size of his strongly knit and muscular limbs. Alas, this is a child, a feeble dwarf! It cannot be true that this weak and wrinkled shrimp strikes such terror in his enemies."

Hercules was an enormously strong PanHellenic hero, famous for the labors he performed in the ancient world. Hector was the greatest Trojan warrior during the Trojan War.

"Madam, I have been bold to trouble you," Lord Talbot said. "But since your ladyship is not at leisure, I'll arrange some other time to visit you."

He turned to leave.

"What is he doing?" the Countess of Auvergne asked. "Go and ask him where he is going."

"Stay, my Lord Talbot," the messenger said, "for my lady wants to know the reason for your abrupt departure."

"I want to show her that she is mistaken," Lord Talbot said. "I go to certify to her that Talbot is here."

The Countess of Auvergne thought that Lord Talbot was unimpressive. He was leaving to show her that he in fact was a man who was in control.

The porter came back. He had done his job of locking the gate to the courtyard.

The Countess of Auvergne said, "If you are Talbot, then you are a prisoner."

"A prisoner!" Lord Talbot said. "To whom?"

"To me, bloodthirsty lord," the Countess of Auvergne said. "That is the reason I lured you to my house. For a long time your shadow — your appearance — has been a captive to me, for in my gallery your picture hangs. But now the substance — the real man — shall endure the same captivity, and I will chain these legs and arms of yours that have by tyranny these many years wasted our country, slain our citizens, and sent our sons and husbands into captivity."

Lord Talbot laughed.

"Are you laughing, wretch?" the Countess of Auvergne said. "Your laughing shall change to moaning."

Lord Talbot said, "I laugh to see that your ladyship is so foolish as to think that you have anything other than Talbot's shadow on which to practice your cruelty."

"Why, aren't you Talbot?" the Countess of Auvergne asked.

"I am indeed."

"Then I have your substance as well as your shadow."

"No, no," Talbot said. "I am only the shadow of myself. You are deceived; my substance is not here, for what you see in front of you is only the smallest part and least proportion of manhood. I tell you, madam, that if the whole frame were here, it is of such a spacious lofty height, your roof were not sufficiently high to contain it."

He meant that although he was the leader of the English army, he was only a small part of that army. He may have been the head of the army, but the army was the body. His army was much too large for the Countess of Auvergne's castle to contain.

The Countess of Auvergne said, "This man is a purveyor of riddles for the occasion. Talbot is here, and yet he is not here. How can these contradictory facts agree?"

"I will show you that right now," Lord Talbot said.

He blew his horn. Military drums started playing, and a cannon fired a cannonball through the courtyard gate. Armed English soldiers rushed into the room.

"What do you say now, madam?" Lord Talbot said. "Are you now persuaded that Talbot is only a shadow of himself? These are his substance, sinews, arms, and strength with which he yokes and makes submit your rebellious necks, razes your cities, and destroys your towns and in a moment makes them desolate."

"Victorious Talbot!" the Countess of Auvergne said. "Pardon my deception. I find that you are no less than your fame and reputation have proclaimed you to be and that you are more than may be gathered by your shape. Let my presumption not provoke your wrath, for I am sorry that I did not treat you with reverence as you are."

"Be not dismayed, fair lady," Lord Talbot said. "And do not misconstrue the mind of Talbot, as you misconstrued the outward composition of his body. What you have done has not offended me, and I do not crave other satisfaction except only, with your permission, that we may taste your wine and see what delicacies you have, for soldiers' stomachs always serve them well."

The Countess of Auvergne replied, "With all my heart, and believe that I am honored to feast so great a warrior in my house."

In a garden with rose bushes, some bearing red roses and some bearing white roses, near the Middle and Inner Temples in London, the Duke of Somerset, the Earl of Suffolk, and the Earl of Warwick stood, along with Richard Plantagenet, Vernon, and another lawyer: six people in all. The Temples were areas devoted to the study and practice of law, and Richard Plantagenet and the Duke of Somerset had been disputing a point of law.

Richard Plantagenet and the Duke of Somerset were both members of royal families, being descended from King Edward III, but Richard Plantagenet was a member of the York family and the Duke of Somerset was a member of the Lancaster family.

King Henry V died on 31 August 1422. In future years, from 1455-1487, the Yorkists and the Lancastrians would fight for power in England in the famous Wars of the Roses. The emblem of the York family would be a white rose, and the emblem of the Lancaster family would be a red rose.

Richard Plantagenet asked, "Great lords and gentlemen, what means this silence? Dare no man answer in a case of truth?"

The Earl of Suffolk said, "Within the Temple Hall we would have been too loud. The garden here is more suitable for our discussion."

Richard Plantagenet replied, "Then say at once whether I maintained the truth, or wrangling Somerset was in the wrong."

This was a version of "Heads I win, tails you lose."

The Earl of Suffolk replied, "Truly, I have been a truant in the law and have been neglectful in my study of it. I have never been able to frame — that is, train — my will to study law, and therefore I frame — that is, adapt — the law to my will."

The Duke of Somerset said, "My Lord of Warwick, then, you judge between us."

The Earl of Warwick replied, "Between two hawks, which flies the higher height; between two dogs, which has the deeper bark; between two sword blades, which bears the better temper; between two horses, which carries himself best; between two girls, which has the merriest eye, I have perhaps some shallow spirit of judgment, but in these precise and sharp hair-splitting quibbles of the law, I have to say in good faith that I am no wiser than a jackdaw."

A jackdaw was reputed to be a foolish bird.

"Tut, tut, here is a mannerly forbearance," Richard Plantagenet said. "This is a well-mannered refusal to get involved and commit oneself, but the truth appears so naked on my side that any half-blind eye may see it."

The Duke of Somerset said, "And on my side the truth is so well appareled, so clear, so shining, and so evident that it will glimmer through a blind man's eye and he will see it."

Richard Plantagenet said to the men being asked to judge the dispute, "Since you are tongue-tied and so loath to speak, proclaim your thoughts in silent symbols. Let him who is a true-born gentleman and stands upon the honor of his birth pluck a white rose with me from off this rose brier if he thinks that I have pleaded the truth."

The Duke of Somerset said, "Let him who is no coward and who is no flatterer, but who dares to maintain the party of the truth, pluck a red rose from off this rose briar with me."

The Earl of Warwick, knowing that white was not considered a color, said, "I love no colors, and without all color — appearance — of base, low, fawning flattery, I pluck this white rose with Richard Plantagenet."

The Earl of Suffolk said, "I pluck this red rose with young Somerset and say by doing so I think he is in the right."

Vernon said, "Wait, lords and gentlemen, and pluck no more roses, until you decide that he upon whose side the fewest roses are cropped from the bushes shall yield to the other and say that he has the right opinion."

The Duke of Somerset said, "Good Master Vernon, it is a good idea. If I have fewer roses plucked in support of me, I will agree that the other person — Richard Plantagenet — is in the right and I will be silent and no longer object."

Richard Plantagenet said, "I will do the same."

Vernon said, "Then for the truth and plainness of the case, I pluck this pale and maiden blossom here, giving my verdict on the white-rose side."

The Duke of Somerset said, "Don't prick your finger as you pluck the white rose off the bush, lest by bleeding on it you paint the white rose red and thereby fall on my side against your will."

Vernon replied, "If I, my lord, bleed for my opinion, aka my judgment, then opinion, aka my reputation, which is based on my character, shall be the surgeon to my injury and keep me on the side where I still am."

The Duke of Somerset said, "Well, well, come on. Who else needs to pluck a rose?"

The lawyer said, "Unless my study and my books are mistaken, the argument you held was wrong in you, and in sign thereof I pluck a white rose, too."

Four people held white roses: Richard Plantagenet, the Earl of Warwick, Vernon, and the lawyer.

Only two people held red roses: The Duke of Somerset and the Earl of Suffolk.

Richard Plantagenet said, "Now, Duke of Somerset, where is your argument?"

"Here in my scabbard, thinking about doing something that shall dye your white rose a bloody red," the Duke of Somerset replied.

Richard Plantagenet said, "In the meantime your cheeks imitate our white roses because they look pale with fear, as if they were witnessing that the truth is on our side."

"No, Plantagenet," the Duke of Somerset said, "my cheeks are not pale because of fear but because of anger, and your red cheeks blush for pure shame to imitate our roses, and yet your tongue will not confess your error."

"Doesn't your rose have a cankerworm eating it, Duke of Somerset?"

"Doesn't your rose have a thorn, Plantagenet?"

"Yes," Richard Plantagenet said, "and the thorn is sharp and piercing, to protect its truth, while your consuming cankerworm eats its falsehood."

The Duke of Somerset said, "Well, I'll find friends to wear my bleeding roses, and they shall maintain what I have said is true where false, perfidious Plantagenet dare not be seen."

Richard Plantagenet replied, "Now, by this maiden — white — blossom in my hand, I scorn thee and your fashion, peevish boy."

Richard Plantagenet insultingly used the word "thee" to refer to the Duke of Somerset. The words "peevish" and "boy" were also insulting.

The Earl of Suffolk, who supported the Duke of Somerset, said, "Don't turn your scorns this way, Plantagenet."

The Earl of Suffolk's name was William de la Pole.

Richard Plantagenet said to him, "Proud Pole, I will, and I scorn both him and thee."

"I'll turn my part of that scorn into your throat," the Earl of Suffolk said.

"Let's go, let's go, good William de la Pole!" the Duke of Somerset said. "We show grace to the yeoman by conversing with him."

Calling Richard Plantagenet a "yeoman" was another insult. A "yeoman" was not a noble. Richard Plantagenet came from a noble family, but his father had been executed for treason by order of King Henry V and as a result Richard Plantagenet had lost his land and his noble titles.

The Earl of Warwick said, "Now, by God's will, you wrong him, Duke of Somerset. His grandfather was Lionel, Duke of Clarence, who was the third son to Edward III, King of England. Do crestless yeomen spring from so deep a root?"

A crest is a part of a heraldic display and sits on top of the helmet.

Richard Plantagenet said, "He knows about this place's privilege — no violence is allowed here. If not for that, he would not dare, for all his cowardly heart, to say this."

"By Him Who made me, on any plot of ground in Christendom I'll maintain my words are true," the Duke of Somerset said. "Wasn't your father, Richard, Earl of Cambridge, executed for treason in the reign of our late King Henry V? And, because of his treason, don't you stand tainted, deprived of your titles, and excluded from ancient gentry — long-established high rank? His trespass — his treason — yet lives on guilty in your blood, and until you are restored to your titles, you are a yeoman, a commoner."

Richard Plantagenet replied, "My father was arrested, not attainted. He was condemned to die for treason, but he was no traitor. And I will prove that in a trial of combat on better men than you, Duke of Somerset, when I have the opportunity."

He meant that his father had been arrested and executed for treason by the order of King Henry V; this had not been done by a full bill of attainder in Parliament and so his father had not been attainted. A bill of attainder is a legislative bill declaring a person or a group of people guilty of crime and ordering punishment for the crime.

Richard Plantagenet continued, "As for your associate William de la Pole and you yourself, I'll note you in my book of memory so that I remember to scourge you for this opinion. Look to see it happen and say you are well warned."

The Duke of Somerset replied, "Ah, you shall find us ready for thee always, and you will know us by these colors — we will wear the red rose — for your foes, for my friends shall wear the red rose in defiance of thee."

Richard Plantagenet said, "And, by my soul, this pale and angry rose, as a sign of my bloodthirsty and blood-drinking hate, I and my faction will forever wear, until it withers with me in my grave or it flourishes to the height of my rank and standing."

The Earl of Suffolk said, "Go forward and be choked with your ambition! And so farewell until I meet thee next."

The Earl of Suffolk, aka William de la Pole, exited.

The Duke of Somerset said, "I'll go with you, William de la Pole. Farewell, ambitious Richard."

The Duke of Somerset exited.

Richard Plantagenet said, "How I am defied and insulted and must necessarily endure it!"

The Earl of Warwick said, "This blot that they object against your house shall be wiped out in the next Parliament, which has been called to make a truce between the Bishop of Winchester and the Duke of Gloucester. If you are not then made the Duke of York, I will not live to be considered the Earl of Warwick. You are as likely not to gain the title of Duke of York as I am to lose my title. In the meantime, as a sign of my love and friendship for you, and in opposition to the proud Duke of Somerset and William de la Pole, I will as a part of your faction wear this white rose. And here I prophesy: This brawl today, grown to this factious quarrel in the Temple garden, shall send between the red rose and the white rose a thousand souls to death and deadly night. Many, many people will die as a result of this quarrel that happened tonight."

Richard Plantagenet said, "Good Master Vernon, I am bound to you because on my behalf you plucked a white rose."

"On your behalf I will always wear a white rose," Vernon said.

"And so will I," the lawyer said.

"Thanks, gentle sir," Richard Plantagenet said. "Come, let us four go to dinner. I dare say that this quarrel will drink blood some day."

44

— 2.5 —

In the Tower of London, Edmund Mortimer, the Earl of March, sat in a chair. With him were some of his jail keepers. He had a claim to the throne, and so King Henry IV had imprisoned him, and King Henry V had continued to imprison him. Now he was old and dying.

Mortimer said, "Kind keepers of my weak, decaying age, let dying Mortimer here rest himself."

The keepers were both jail keepers and caregivers.

He continued, "Just like the limbs of a man recently dragged from off the rack, so fare my limbs with long imprisonment. And these grey locks of hair, the pursuivants — the heralds — of death, argue the arrival of the end of Edmund Mortimer, who is Nestor-like aged in an age of care."

Nestor was the old, wise advisor to the Greek commander Agamemnon and the Greek army during the Trojan War.

Mortimer continued, "My eyes, like lamps whose wasting oil is spent, grow dim, as drawing to their end. My weak shoulders, overborne with burdensome grief, and my pithless, feeble, strengthless arms are like a withered vine that droops its sapless branches to the ground. Yet these feet, whose strengthless support is paralyzed, are unable to support this lump of clay, which is swift-winged with desire to get a grave, as if they know I have no other comfort.

"But tell me, keeper, will my nephew come?"

The first jailer said, "Richard Plantagenet, my lord, will come. We sent to the Temple, to his chamber, and the answer was returned that he will come."

"Good. That is enough," Mortimer replied. "My soul shall then be satisfied. Poor gentleman! The wrong done to him equals mine. Since King Henry V, who was born at Monmouth, first began to reign, before whose glory I was great in arms, this loathsome imprisonment I have endured, and ever since then has Richard Plantagenet been living in obscurity, deprived of honor and inheritance. But now the arbitrator of despair — just death, the kind umpire of men's miseries — with sweet release dismisses me from here. I wish Richard Plantagenet's troubles likewise were ended so that he might recover what was lost."

Richard Plantagenet entered the room.

The first jailer said, "My lord, your loving nephew now has come."

"My friend, has Richard Plantagenet come?" Mortimer asked.

Richard Plantagenet answered, "Yes, noble uncle, thus ignobly used, your nephew, the recently despised and insulted Richard, has come."

Mortimer said to the jailers, "Guide my arms so that I may embrace his neck and on his bosom expend my last gasp. Oh, tell me when my lips touch his cheeks, so that I may affectionately give one fainting kiss."

With the help of his jailers, Mortimer was able to hug and kiss his nephew.

To Richard Plantagenet, he said, "Now declare, sweet branch from York's great tree, why did you say that recently you were despised?"

Richard Plantagenet was a member of the York family while Kings Henry IV, Henry V, and Henry VI were members of the Lancaster family, being descended from John of Gaunt, first Duke of Lancaster. Richard Plantagenet's grandfather was Edmund Langley, Duke of York (1341-1402).

Richard Plantagenet replied, "First, lean your aged back against my arm, and with you in that comfortable position, I'll tell you about my trouble.

"This day, in an argument about a case, some words were exchanged between the Duke of Somerset and me. During the argument he used his lavish tongue to say words that upbraided me with my father's death. This reproach set bars before my tongue, or else with similar abuse I would have requited him. Therefore, good uncle, for my father's sake, in honor of a true Plantagenet and for the sake of kinship, tell me the reason my father, the Earl of Cambridge, was beheaded."

"He was beheaded for the same reason, fair nephew, that imprisoned me and has detained me during all of my flowering youth within a loathsome dungeon, where I pine and grieve. That reason was the cursed instrument of his decease."

"Tell me in more detail what reason that was," Richard Plantagenet said, "because I am ignorant of it and cannot guess."

He knew the reason, but he wanted to hear Mortimer say it.

Mortimer replied, "I will, if my fading breath permits me and if death does not approach me before my tale is done. King Henry IV, grandfather to this King, Henry VI, deposed his cousin Richard II, who was Edward the Black Prince's son, the first-begotten and lawful heir of King Edward III, the third of that descent as well as the third Edward. During King Henry IV's reign, the

Percy family of the north, finding his usurpation most unjust, endeavored to advance me to the throne, hoping to make me King. These warlike lords were moved to attempt to do that because — young King Richard II thus removed, leaving no heir begotten from his body — by birth and parentage, I was the next in line to be King, for by my grandmother I am descended from Lionel, who was both the Duke of Clarence and the third son of King Edward III, whereas he — King Henry IV —gets his pedigree from John of Gaunt. But John of Gaunt was only the fourth son of that heroic line, and so I ought to have been made King.

"But listen carefully. In this lofty, high-minded attempt, the Percy family labored to plant the rightful heir, but I lost my liberty and they lost their lives.

"Long after this, when King Henry V, succeeding his father Henry Bolingbroke, aka King Henry IV, reigned, your father, the Earl of Cambridge, again because of pity for my hard distress levied an army, hoping to rescue me and install me in the throne and have me wear the crown. Your father, who was descended from famous Edmund Langley, Duke of York, had married my sister, who became your mother. But, like the rest, your noble father, the Earl of Cambridge, fell and was beheaded. Thus the Mortimers, in whom the title rested, were suppressed."

"Of the Mortimers," Richard Plantagenet said, "you, your honor, are the last."

"True," Mortimer said, "and you see that I have no children and that my fainting words assure you that I am dying. You are my heir; the rest I wish you to gather."

The word "gather" meant both to "infer" and to "collect." Richard Plantagenet could infer that he ought to be King of England, and he could decide to gather an army and collect the crown.

Mortimer continued, "But always be wary in your studious care."

Attempting to become King of England would be dangerous.

Richard Plantagenet said, "Your grave admonishments prevail with me, but still, I think, my father's execution was nothing less than bloody tyranny."

"Be shrewd, nephew," Mortimer said. "Be shrewd with silence. Strongly fixed is the House of Lancaster — Henry IV, Henry V, and Henry VI were and are Lancastrians — and like a mountain, not to be moved. But now your uncle is dying and thereby removing from here as Princes do their courts, when they are cloyed and satiated with long continuance in a settled place."

"Oh, uncle, I wish some part of my young years might redeem the passage of your age!" Richard Plantagenet said. "I wish I could use some of my years of life to buy back for you some of your years."

Mortimer said, "You would then wrong me, as that slaughterer does who gives many wounds when one will kill. Don't mourn, unless you feel sorrow for my good."

The last sentence is ambiguous. It can mean 1) Don't mourn unless you mourn because the good in me is dying, and 2) Don't mourn unless you use your sorrow to do me good — to get revenge for the wrong done to me.

He continued, "Only give the order and make the arrangements for my funeral, and so farewell, and may all your hopes be fair and may your life be prosperous in peace and war!"

Mortimer died.

Richard Plantagenet said, "And may peace, and no war, befall your parting soul! In prison you spent a pilgrimage and like a hermit passed your days. Well, I will lock his counsel in my breast, and what I am planning — let that rest.

"Keepers, convey him from here, and I myself will see that his burial is better than his life. I will make sure that he receives the honor at his funeral that he was denied during his life."

The jailers carried away Mortimer's corpse.

Richard Plantagenet said, "Here dies the dusky, extinguished torch of Mortimer, choked by the ambition of those who are inferior to him. As for those wrongs and those bitter injuries that the Duke of Somerset has offered to my family, I don't doubt that I will with honor redress them.

"Therefore I now hasten to the Parliament. Either I will be restored to my blood, aka my privileges of noble rank and noble birth that I lost when my father was executed, or I will make my ill the advantage of my good — that is, I will make the injuries done to me fuel my ambition to advance."

CHAPTER 3

— 3.1 —

At the Parliament House in London, several people were meeting: King Henry VI, the Duke of Exeter, the Duke of Gloucester, the Earl of Warwick, the Duke of Somerset, the Earl of Suffolk, the Bishop of Winchester, Richard Plantagenet, and others. The Duke of Gloucester attempted to present an indictment listing accusations against the Bishop of Winchester to the King, but the Bishop of Winchester grabbed it and tore it up.

The Bishop of Winchester said to the Duke of Gloucester, "Have you come with a carefully considered list of accusations you have written in advance? Have you come with studiously devised written documents, Humphrey, you Duke of Gloucester? If you can accuse me or intend to make charges against me of anything, do it without premeditation, do it extempore, as I with unpremeditated and extemporal speech intend to answer whatever you accuse me of."

"Presumptuous priest!" the Duke of Gloucester said. "This place commands my patience and so I have to remain peaceful, or you would find out from my reaction that you have dishonored me. Don't think that although in writing I presented the manner of your vile, outrageous crimes, I have therefore forged lies or am not able verbally to relate the thesis of my pen. No, prelate. Such is your audacious wickedness and your wicked, pestilent, quarrelsome, and malicious deeds that even children prattle about your pride.

"You are a most pernicious usurer, perverse by nature, an enemy to peace; you are lascivious and wanton, more than is well suitable for a man of your profession and degree, and as for your treachery, what's more evident? You laid a trap to take my life at London Bridge as well as at the Tower of London.

"Besides, I am afraid that if your thoughts were carefully examined, the King, your sovereign, is not quite exempt from the spiteful malice of your pride-swollen heart."

The Bishop of Winchester said, "Duke of Gloucester, I defy you. Lords, agree to hear what I shall reply to these charges. If I were covetous, ambitious, or perverse, as he says I am, how is it that I am so poor?"

Actually, the Bishop of Winchester was rich. Some of his income came from usurious loans; some of it came from rent charged to brothels that operated on land he owned.

He continued, "Or how does it happen that I don't seek to advance or raise myself, but keep my wonted calling?"

Actually, the Bishop of Winchester wanted to be installed officially as the Cardinal of Winchester. Earlier, he had been wearing the red robes of a Cardinal despite not being officially installed as Cardinal.

He continued, "And as for dissension, who prefers peace more than I do? Unless I am provoked.

"No, my good lords, these are not the real reasons for our disagreement. These are not the real reasons that the Duke of Gloucester is incensed.

"He is incensed because he believes that no one should rule the country except for himself. He believes that no one but he should be around King Henry VI. This is what engenders thunder in his breast and makes him roar forth these accusations. But he shall know I am as good —"

The Duke of Gloucester interrupted: "— as good! You bastard of my grandfather!"

John of Gaunt was the Duke of Gloucester's grandfather and the Bishop of Winchester's father. When Catherine Swynford gave birth to the Bishop of Winchester, she and John of Gaunt were not married, although they married later.

"Yes, lordly sir," the Bishop of Winchester said, "but what are you, I ask, other than one acting imperiously in another's throne?"

"Am I not the Lord Protector, saucy priest?"

"And am not I a prelate of the church?"

"Yes, as an outlaw dwells in a castle and uses it to maintain his thievery," the Duke of Gloucester said.

"Irreverent Gloucester!" the Bishop of Winchester said.

"You are reverent when it comes to your spiritual function — your profession — but not when it comes to your life."

"The Pope shall make you pay for this," the Bishop of Winchester said. "Rome shall remedy this."

"Roam thither, then," the Duke of Gloucester said.

In the quarrel, the Earl of Warwick took the side of the Duke of Gloucester, and the Duke of Somerset took the side of the Bishop of Winchester.

"Bishop of Winchester, my lord, it is your duty to forbear and control yourself," the Earl of Warwick said.

"Yes," the Duke of Somerset said, "as long as the Bishop of Winchester is not borne down and bullied by superior force. I think my lord the Duke of Gloucester should be religious and know and respect the office that belongs to such as are religious."

"I think his lordship the Bishop of Winchester should be humbler," the Earl of Warwick said. "It is not suitable for a prelate to contend in debate in this way."

"Yes, it is, when his holy state is affected so directly," the Duke of Somerset said. "His ecclesiastical status is under attack."

"Whether his state is holy or unhallowed, so what?" the Earl of Warwick said. "Isn't his grace the Duke of Gloucester Lord Protector to the King?"

Richard Plantagenet thought, *Plantagenet, I see, must hold his tongue, lest it be said, "Speak, sirrah, when you should; must your bold verdict enter talk with lords?" Otherwise, I would fling words at the Bishop of Winchester.*

Richard Plantagenet knew that his social status was not high enough for him to be allowed to speak up and express his opinion in this quarrel.

King Henry VI, who was young, said, "Uncle of Gloucester and great-uncle of Winchester, you two are the special watchmen of our English commonwealth. I would prevail, if prayers might prevail, and join your hearts in love and amity. Oh, what a scandal it is to our crown that two such noble peers as you should quarrel!

"Believe me, lords, my tender years can tell that civil dissension is a venomous snake that gnaws the bowels of the commonwealth."

People in this culture incorrectly believed that vipers were born by gnawing their way out of the body of their mother.

Someone shouted outside the room, "Down with the tawny-coats!"

King Henry VI asked, "What disturbance is this?"

The Earl of Warwick replied, "It is an uproar, I dare guess, that has begun through the malice of the Bishop of Winchester's men."

Someone shouted outside the room, "Stones! Stones!"

The Mayor of London entered the room and said, "Oh, my good lords, and virtuous Henry, pity the city of London. Pity us! The Bishop of Winchester's men and the Duke of Gloucester's men, who were recently forbidden to carry any weapons, have filled their pockets full of small stones. Banding themselves into opposing sides, they throw stones so hard at each other's heads that many have had their giddy, angry brains knocked out. Our windows and shutters are broken in every street, and out of fear we are compelled to shut our shops."

Some serving men with bloody heads, fighting, entered the room. Some were wearing blue coats; some were wearing tawny coats.

Using the royal plural, King Henry VI said, "We order you, on your allegiance to ourself, to restrain your slaughtering hands and keep the peace.

"Please, uncle Duke of Gloucester, pacify this strife."

The first serving man, who served the Duke of Gloucester, said, "If we are forbidden to fight with stones, we'll use our teeth as weapons."

The second serving man, who served the Bishop of Winchester, replied, "Do whatever you dare to do, for we are as resolute as you."

The serving men fought again.

The Duke of Gloucester said, "You who are of my household, leave this foolish disturbance and set this unusual fight aside."

The third serving man said, "My lord, we know your grace to be a man who is just and upright, and as for your royal birth, it is inferior to none but to his majesty. Therefore, before we will suffer such a Prince as yourself, so kind a father of the commonwealth, to be disgraced by an inkhorn mate — the Latin-writing Bishop of Winchester — we and our wives and children all will fight and have our bodies slaughtered by your foes."

The first serving man said, "Yes, and the very parings of our nails shall be sharp stakes to be used to fortify a battlefield when we are dead."

The two groups of serving men started fighting again.

"Stop! Stop, I say!" the Duke of Gloucester said. "If you love me, as you say you do, let me persuade you to stop fighting for awhile."

"Oh, how this discord afflicts my soul!" the young King Henry VI said. "Can you, my Lord of Winchester, see my sighs and tears and yet you will not at once relent? Who should take pity on me, if you do not? Who would endeavor to prefer peace to war if holy churchmen take delight in quarrels?"

The Earl of Warwick advised both sides to make peace: "Yield, my Lord Protector, Duke of Gloucester; yield, Bishop of Winchester. Yield and make peace, unless you intend with an obstinate refusal to make peace to slay your sovereign and destroy the realm. You see what evil and what murder, too, have been enacted through your enmity; so then, be at peace unless you thirst for blood."

"He shall submit, or I will never yield," the Bishop of Winchester said.

"Compassion for the King compels me to stoop," the Duke of Gloucester said. "Otherwise, I would see the Bishop of Winchester's heart out of his body, before the priest should ever get that privilege of me."

"That privilege of me" was ambiguous. The sentence it appears in could mean 1) "Otherwise, I would see the Bishop of Winchester's heart out of his body, before the priest should ever get my heart out of my body" or 2) "Otherwise, I would see the Bishop of Winchester's heart out of his body, before the priest should ever get me to humble myself first."

The Earl of Warwick said, "Look, my Lord of Winchester, the Duke of Gloucester has banished his moody, discontented fury, as is shown by his smoothed forehead. Why do you still look so stern and sorrowful?"

"Here, Bishop of Winchester, I offer you my hand," the Duke of Gloucester said, holding out his hand.

The Bishop of Winchester, whose name was Henry Beaufort, did not take it.

"Shame on you, great-uncle Beaufort!" King Henry VI said. "I have heard you preach that malice is a great and grievous sin, and now you will not maintain the thing you teach, but instead you will show yourself to be a chief offender in the same?"

The Earl of Warwick said, "Sweet King! The Bishop of Winchester has received a suitable rebuke! For shame, my lord of Winchester, relent! What, shall a child teach you how to act?"

The Bishop of Winchester said, "Well, Duke of Gloucester, I will yield to you. Love for your love and hand for your hand I give."

They shook hands.

The Duke of Gloucester thought, *Yes, but I am afraid that you are shaking my hand with a false heart. You don't really mean to make peace with me.*

He said out loud, "See here, my friends and loving countrymen, this handshake serves as a flag of truce between ourselves and all our followers. So help me, God, I am not lying!"

The Bishop of Winchester thought, *So help me, God, I don't intend there to be peace between the Duke of Gloucester and me!*

King Henry VI said, "Oh, loving uncle, kind Duke of Gloucester, how joyful I am made by this contract of peace!"

He said to the serving men who had been quarreling, "Go away, my masters! Trouble us no more, but join in friendship, as your lords have done."

The first serving man said, "I am happy with this peace agreement. I'll go now to see a doctor."

The second serving man said, "And so will I."

The third serving man said, "And I will see what 'medicine' I can get at the tavern."

The serving men and the Mayor of London exited.

The Earl of Warwick gave a document to King Henry VI and said, "Accept this scroll, most gracious sovereign, which in support of the claim of Richard Plantagenet we give to your majesty so that you may consider it."

The Duke of Gloucester said, "Well urged, my Lord of Warwick, because, sweet King, if your grace notes every detail, you have great reason to do Richard Plantagenet right, especially for those reasons I told your majesty at Eltham Place."

"And those reasons, uncle, were very persuasive," King Henry VI said. "Therefore, my loving lords, our pleasure is that Richard Plantagenet be restored to his hereditary rights and title."

The Earl of Warwick said, "As the King said, let Richard Plantagenet be restored to his hereditary rights and title. In this way, his father's wrongs shall receive recompense."

The Bishop of Winchester said, "What the other lords want, so also do I, the Bishop of Winchester, want."

King Henry VI said, "If Richard Plantagenet will be loyal, not just that alone will I give to him, but also all the whole inheritance that belongs to the House of York, from whence you spring by lineal descent."

Richard Plantagenet pledged his loyalty to the King: "Your humble servant vows obedience and humble service until I reach the point of death."

King Henry VI replied, "Stoop then and set your knee against my foot, and in recompense for that duty you have just performed, I gird you with the valiant sword of York. Rise, Richard, like a true Plantagenet, and rise as the newly created and Princely Duke of York."

Richard Plantagenet, now the Duke of York, said, "And may I, Richard, thrive as your foes fall! May your enemies die and I thrive! And as my duty flourishes, so may they who think even one complaining thought against your majesty die!"

All said, "Welcome, high Prince, the mighty Duke of York!"

The Duke of Somerset thought, *Perish, base Prince, ignoble Duke of York!*

The Duke of Gloucester said to King Henry VI, "Now will it best avail your majesty to cross the seas and to be crowned in France. The presence of a King engenders love among his subjects and his loyal friends as it dismays his enemies."

King Henry V had made a treaty that made the King of England the next King of France. Because the then-King of France died two months after King Henry V had died, King Henry VI of England was regarded — by the English — as the King of France.

Of course, Charles the Dauphin and Joan la Pucelle disagreed.

King Henry VI replied, "When the Duke of Gloucester says the word, King Henry to France goes, for friendly counsel cuts off many foes."

The Duke of Gloucester said, "Your ships are already prepared for the journey."

Everyone except the Duke of Exeter left the room.

Alone, the Duke of Exeter said to himself, "Yes, we may march in England or in France, not seeing what is likely to ensue. This recent dissension grown between the Duke of Gloucester and the Bishop of Winchester burns under feigned ashes of forged love and will at last break out into a flame."

The Duke of Exeter was aware that the quarrel between the Duke of Gloucester and the Bishop of Winchester had not been truly resolved. It was like the coals of a fire burning under ashes; the coals could soon burst into open flame.

He continued, "As festering limbs rot bit by bit until bones and flesh and sinews fall away, so will this base and envious discord grow. And now I fear that fatal prophecy which in the time of King Henry V was in the mouth of every sucking babe: Henry born at Monmouth — that is, Henry V — would win all, and Henry born at Windsor — that is, Henry VI — would lose all. King Henry V won many cities in France, and according to the prophecy, King Henry VI will lose all of those cities. The truth of this prophecy is so plain that I, the Duke of Exeter, wishes that his days may end before that hapless time. I hope to die before I see the prophecy come true."

— 3.2 —

The English held the city of Rouen, but Joan la Pucelle had a plan to enable the French army to retake the city. She and four French soldiers stood in front of one of the entrances into the city. Joan and the soldiers were carrying sacks of wheat on their backs.

Joan la Pucelle said, "These are the city gates, the gates of Rouen, through which we must make a breach by use of a stratagem. Take heed, and be wary how you express your words. Talk like the vulgar sort of market men who come to gather money for their wheat. If we have entrance, as I hope we shall, and if we find the slothful watch weak, I'll by a sign give notice to our friends that Charles the Dauphin may kill the watchmen and enter the city."

The first soldier said, "Our sacks shall be a means by which we can sack the city, and we will be lords and rulers over Rouen. Therefore we'll knock."

The first soldier knocked.

An English watchman asked, "*Qui la?*"

"*Qui la?*" means "Who there?"

The English watchman knew a little French, but not enough to know to say, "*Qui est la?*"

"*Qui est la?*" means "Who is there?"

Joan la Pucelle said, "*Paysans, pauvres gens de France.*"

This means "Peasants, the poor tribe of France."

Realizing that English watchman did not know much French, Joan la Pucelle added this sentence in English: "Poor market folks who come to sell their wheat."

The English watchman said, "Enter, go in; the market bell has been rung."

Joan la Pucelle said to herself, "Now, Rouen, I'll shake your bulwarks to the ground."

She and the four disguised French soldiers went through the gate into the city.

Charles the Dauphin, the Bastard of Orleans, the Duke of Alençon, Reignier, and some soldiers arrived and stood outside the gate.

Charles the Dauphin said, "May Saint Denis bless this happy stratagem and make it successful! If he does, once again we'll sleep securely in Rouen."

The Bastard of Orleans said, "Pucelle and her co-conspirators entered the city here through this gate. Now she is there, how will she specify where is the best and safest passage into the city

Reignier replied, "By thrusting out a torch from yonder tower. Once the torch is discerned, it will show that her meaning is that no entrance to the city is weaker than this one through which she entered."

Joan la Pucelle appeared on the tower and displayed a burning torch.

She said, "Behold, this is the happy wedding torch that joins Rouen to her countrymen, but this torch's burning is fatal to the Talbonites!"

The word "Talbonites" meant "the followers of Talbot"; the word used a Latinization of "Talbot."

She exited.

The Bastard of Orleans said, "See, noble Charles, the beacon of our friend. The burning torch in yonder tower stands."

Charles the Dauphin said, "Now let it shine like a comet of revenge, a portent prophesying to us the fall of all our foes!"

"Waste no time," Reignier said. "Delays have dangerous ends. Enter, and cry 'The Dauphin!' immediately, and then kill the watchmen."

A battle trumpet sounded and they entered the city and began fighting.

Talbot appeared and said, "France, you shall rue this treason with your tears, if I, Talbot, can survive your treachery."

To the English, King Henry VI was also King of France, and so the French who were battling to take the city of Rouen were traitors.

Talbot continued, "Pucelle, that witch, that damned sorceress, has wrought this Hellish and wicked deed without warning, so that only with difficulty did we escape the haughty power of France."

Then he began to fight again.

As the fighting continued, the Duke of Bedford was carried in a chair to a place where he could watch the fighting. The Duke of Bedford was ill; in fact, he was dying.

The French took the city. Talbot and the Duke of Burgundy left the city and stood together outside by the Duke of Bedford. On the wall of Rouen stood Joan la Pucelle, Charles the Dauphin, the Bastard of Orleans, the Duke of Alençon, and Reignier.

Joan la Pucelle taunted the English: "Good morning, gallants! Do you want wheat for bread?"

She threw grains of wheat at the English.

She added, "I think the Duke of Burgundy will fast before he'll buy again at such a rate. It was full of darnel; do you like the taste?"

Darnel is a weed that commonly grows among stalks of wheat.

The Duke of Burgundy said, "Scoff on, vile fiend and shameless courtesan! I trust before long to choke you with your own wheat and make you curse the harvest of that wheat."

Charles the Dauphin said, "Your grace may starve perhaps before that time."

The Duke of Bedford said, "Let no words, but deeds, revenge this treason!"

"What will you do, good grey-beard?" Joan la Pucelle said, "Break a lance, engage in a jousting match, and charge at death while you sit in a chair?"

Talbot said, "Foul fiend of France, and hag of all malice and spite, you are surrounded by your lustful paramours! Does it become and suit you to taunt the Duke of Bedford's valiant age and twit in a cowardly way a man who is half dead? Damsel, I'll have a bout with you again, or else let Talbot perish with this shame."

The word "bout" could mean a bout of fighting or a bout of sex.

Punning on the word "hot" as meaning "angry" and "horny," Joan la Pucelle said, "Are ye so hot, sir? Yet, Pucelle, hold your peace. If Talbot do but thunder, rain will follow."

The English whispered together in a council.

Joan la Pucelle said, "May God speed the Parliament! Who shall be the Speaker of the Parliament?"

"Do you dare to come forth and meet us on the battlefield?" Talbot asked, challenging them to a battle.

Joan la Pucelle said, "It is likely that your lordship takes us then for fools who are willing to fight a risky battle to get what they have already won."

Talbot said, "I speak not to that railing Hecate — that witch — but to you, Duke of Alençon, and to the rest. Will you, like soldiers, come and fight it out?"

Hecate was an ancient Greek goddess who protected witches.

The Duke of Alençon replied to Talbot, "Signior, no."

"Signior, hang!" Talbot shouted. "Base muleteers of France! Like peasant footboys they keep behind the wall and dare not take up arms and fight like gentlemen."

"Let's leave, Captains!" Joan la Pucelle said. "Let's get away from the wall, for Talbot means us no goodness by his looks."

She shouted to Talbot, "May God be with you, my lord! We came here only to tell you that we are here."

Joan la Pucelle and the others departed from the wall.

Talbot said, "And there will we be, too, before long, or else may reproach be Talbot's greatest fame! If we don't retake the city, and soon, let me be remembered as a loser.

"Vow, Duke of Burgundy, by the honor of your house, pricked on by public wrongs sustained in France either to get the town again or die."

The Duke of Burgundy was French, but he supported the English.

Talbot continued, "And I, as sure as English Henry VI lives and as sure as his father, Henry V, was conqueror here, and as sure as in this recently betrayed town great Coeur-de-lion's heart was buried, as sure as these things I swear to get the town or die."

King Henry V had captured the town of Rouen in 1418.

King Richard I, known as Coeur-de-lion or Lionheart, had willed that his heart be buried in Rouen because he so loved and respected the town. He died in 1199 in France, and the rest of his body was buried in Fontevrault.

The Duke of Burgundy said, "My vows are equal partners with your vows. I vow the same thing you do."

"But, before we go, let's take care of this dying Prince, the valiant Duke of Bedford," Talbot said. "Come, my lord, we will take you to some better place that is fitter for sickness and for infirm old age."

The Duke of Bedford replied, "Lord Talbot, do not dishonor me so. Here I will sit before the wall of Rouen, and I will be partner of your weal or woe."

The Duke of Burgundy said, "Courageous Duke of Bedford, let us now persuade you —"

The Duke of Bedford interrupted, "— not to be gone from hence, for once I read that brave Uther Pendragon, the father of King Arthur, while sick was carried in a litter to the battlefield and vanquished his foes. I think my being here should revive the soldiers' hearts because I always identified with them."

Talbot said, "You have an undaunted spirit in a dying breast! Then so be it. May the Heavens keep the old Duke of Bedford safe! And now no more ado, brave Duke of Burgundy, but we will gather our forces out of hand and set upon and fight our boasting enemy."

All exited except for the Duke of Bedford and some attendants.

The battle began. Sir John Fastolfe and a Captain came into view. True to his last name, which was similar to Fast-off, Sir John was running away.

The Captain asked, "Where are you going, Sir John Fastolfe, in such haste?"

"Where am I going?" Sir John Fastolfe said. "To save myself by flight. We are likely to be defeated again."

"What!" the Captain said. "Will you flee, and leave Lord Talbot?"

"Yes," Sir John Fastolfe replied. "I would leave all the Talbots in the world in order to save my life!"

He ran away.

Cowardly knight!" the Captain said. "May ill fortune follow you!"

The Captain exited.

The battle continued, and the French lost. Joan la Pucelle, the Duke of Alençon, and Charles the Dauphin fled.

The Duke of Bedford, seeing their flight, said to himself, "Now, quiet soul, depart when it pleases Heaven, for I have seen our enemies' overthrow. What is the trust or strength of foolish man? They who recently were daring with their scoffs are now glad and happy by flight to save themselves."

The Duke of Bedford died, and his attendants carried him away in his chair.

Lord Talbot, the Duke of Burgundy, and others met and discussed their victory.

Lord Talbot, elated, said, "Lost, and recovered again on the same day! This is a double honor, Burgundy. It is an honor for you and for me. Yet the Heavens have the glory for this victory!"

The Duke of Burgundy replied, "Warlike and martial Talbot, I, the Duke of Burgundy, enshrine you in my heart and there erect your noble deeds as monuments of valor."

"Thanks, gentle Duke," Talbot said. "But where is Joan la Pucelle now? I think her old familiar is asleep."

Witches have familiars: attendant spirits in the form of an animal.

Talbot continued, "Now where are the Bastard's boasts and Charles' insults? Are the Bastard and Charles the Dauphin all dejected and downcast?"

He said sarcastically, "Rouen hangs her head for grief because such a 'valiant' company has fled."

He added, "Now we will make arrangements to restore some order in the town, placing therein some expert officers, and then depart to go to Paris and see the King, for in Paris young King Henry VI is staying with his nobles."

The Duke of Burgundy said, "Whatever Lord Talbot wants pleases me, the Duke of Burgundy."

Talbot said, "But yet, before we go, let's not forget the recently deceased noble Duke of Bedford — let's see that his funeral rites are fulfilled in Rouen. A braver soldier never brought his lance down to the attack position, a gentler heart never governed in court, but Kings and the mightiest potentates must die, for that's the end of human misery."

On the plains near Rouen, Charles the Dauphin, the Bastard of Orleans, the Duke of Alençon, and Joan la Pucelle talked. Some soldiers were present.

Joan la Pucelle said, "Princes, don't be dismayed at this event, nor grieve that Rouen has been recovered like this. Care — that is, grief — is no cure, but instead it is corrosive, for things that are not to be remedied. Let wildly enraged Talbot triumph for a while and like a peacock sweep and flaunt his tail; we'll pull his plumes and take away his train — his peacock tail and his army — if Charles the Dauphin and the rest will just take my advice."

Charles the Dauphin said, "We have been guided by you hitherto, and we did not mistrust your cunning. One sudden setback shall never breed distrust. We will continue to trust in you."

The Bastard of Orleans said, "Search your mind for secret stratagems, and we will make you famous throughout the world."

The Duke of Alençon said, "We'll set up your statue in some holy place and have you reverenced like a blessed saint. Therefore, sweet virgin, devote yourself to our good."

Joan la Pucelle said, "Then thus it must be; this is Joan's plan: By fair persuasive arguments mixed with sugared words, we will entice the Duke of Burgundy to leave the Talbot and to follow us."

Charles the Dauphin said, "Yes, indeed, sweet thing, if we could do that, France would be no place for Henry's warriors, nor would England boast to us that France belongs to it, but instead the English would be rooted out from our provinces."

The Duke of Alençon said, "The English would be expelled forever from France and not have the possession of an Earldom here."

Joan la Pucelle said, "Your honors shall perceive how I will work to bring this matter to the wished-for end."

Drums sounded. They were drums first of Talbot's army and second of the Duke of Burgundy's army.

Joan la Pucelle said, "Listen! By the sound of the drums, you may perceive that their armies are marching toward Paris."

The drums of Talbot's army sounded as the English soldiers marched past.

Joan la Pucelle said, "There goes the Talbot, with his flags unfurled, and all the troops of English soldiers after him."

The drums of the Duke of Burgundy's army sounded as the French soldiers in his army marched near Joan and the others.

Joan of Pucelle said, "Now in the rearward come the Duke of Burgundy and his soldiers. Lady Fortune favors us and makes him lag behind. Summon a parley; we will talk with him."

Trumpets sounded a parley.

Charles the Dauphin called, "We wish to have a parley with the Duke of Burgundy!"

The Duke of Burgundy asked, "Who craves a parley with the Burgundy?"

Joan la Pucelle replied, "The Princely Charles of France, your countryman."

"What do you have to say, Charles?" the Duke of Burgundy asked, "I am marching away from here."

"Speak, Pucelle," Charles the Dauphin said, "and enchant him with your words."

Joan la Pucelle said, "Brave Burgundy, undoubted hope of France! Wait, let your humble handmaid speak to you."

"Speak on," the Duke of Burgundy said, "but don't be over-tedious. Don't be too talkative."

Joan la Pucelle said, "Look on your country; look on fertile France, and see the cities and the towns defaced by the wasting ruination wrought by the cruel foe. Just like the mother looks on her lowly babe when death closes his tender, dying eyes, see, see the pining malady of France. Behold the wounds, the most unnatural wounds, which you yourself have given her woeful breast. Oh, turn your edged sword another way! Strike those who hurt France, and do not hurt those who help France. One drop of blood drawn from your country's bosom should grieve you more than streams of foreign gore. Return therefore to the side of France with a flood of tears, and wash away your country's stained spots."

"Either she has bewitched me with her words, or natural feelings make me suddenly relent," the Duke of Burgundy said to himself.

Joan la Pucelle continued, "Besides, all the French and all France exclaim to you, doubting your birth and lawful descent. Who have you joined with but a lordly nation who will not trust you except for the sake of profit? When Talbot has once established firm footing in France and made you a tool of evil, who then but English Henry VI will be lord? You will then be thrust out like a fugitive! We remember, and you should note this as good evidence — wasn't the Duke of Orleans your foe? And wasn't he held prisoner in England? But when they heard he was your enemy, they set him free without his ransom paid, to spite you, Duke of Burgundy, and all your friends. See, then, you are fighting against your countrymen and you have joined with those who will be your slaughterers.

"Come, come, return; return, you wandering lord. Charles the Dauphin and the others will take you in their arms."

"I am vanquished," the Duke of Burgundy said. "These high-minded words of hers have battered me like roaring cannon-shot, and made me almost yield upon my knees.

"Forgive me, country, and sweet countrymen; lords, accept this hearty, heartfelt, kind embrace. My forces and my army of men are yours.

"So farewell, Talbot; I'll no longer trust you."

Joan la Pucelle thought, cynically, *Done like a Frenchman; turn, and turn again! First he fights on one side, and then he fights on the other side!*

"Welcome, brave Duke of Burgundy!" Charles the Dauphin said. "Your friendship invigorates us."

The Bastard of Orleans said, "And it begets new courage in our breasts."

"Joan la Pucelle has bravely played her part in this, and she deserves a coronet of gold," the Duke of Alençon said.

"Now let us continue on, my lords, and join our armies," Charles the Dauphin said, "and seek how we may injure the foe."

At the palace in Paris were King Henry VI, the Duke of Gloucester, the Bishop of Winchester, the Duke of York, the Earl of Suffolk, the Duke of Somerset, the Earl of Warwick, the Duke of Exeter, Vernon, Basset, and others. Lord Talbot was also present, with some soldiers.

Lord Talbot said, "My gracious King, and honorable peers, hearing of your arrival in this realm, I have for awhile given truce to my wars, so that I may express my homage to my sovereign. In sign of that duty, this arm, which has reclaimed to your obedience fifty fortresses, twelve cities, and seven walled towns of strength, besides five hundred prisoners of high rank, lowers the sword it is holding before your highness' feet, and with submissive loyalty of heart I ascribe the glory of the conquests I have gotten first to my God and next unto your grace."

Lord Talbot knelt.

King Henry VI asked, "Uncle Duke of Gloucester, is this the Lord Talbot who has been so long resident in France?"

The Duke of Gloucester replied, "Yes, it is, my liege."

"Welcome, brave Captain and victorious lord!" King Henry VI said to Lord Talbot. "When I was young — I still am not old — I remember how my father said that a braver champion than you never handled a sword. For a long time, we have been aware and completely convinced of your loyalty, your faithful service, and your toil in war, yet never have you tasted our reward, or been recompensed with so much as thanks, because until now we never saw your face. Therefore, stand up, and for these good and worthy deeds of yours, we here make you Earl of Shrewsbury, and in our coronation you will take a place."

Everyone exited except for Vernon and Basset. Vernon was wearing a white rose in support of Richard Plantagenet, the Duke of York; Basset was wearing a red rose in support of the Duke of Somerset. The two men were enemies.

Vernon said to Basset, "Now, sir, to you, who were so hot and angry at sea, insulting this white rose that I wear in honor of my noble Lord of York, do you dare to maintain the former words you spoke?"

"Yes, sir," Basset replied, "as well as you dare to defend the envious barking of your saucy tongue against my lord the Duke of Somerset."

"Sirrah, I honor your lord as he is," Vernon said.

In this context, the word "sirrah" was an insult.

"Why, what is he?" Basset said. "He is as good a man as the Duke of York."

"Listen carefully," Vernon said. "He is not as good a man as the Duke of York."

He struck Basset and said, "As testimony thereof, take that."

Basset said, "Villain, you know the law of arms is such that the penalty is immediate death for whoever draws a sword here, or else this blow should set to flowing your dearest blood."

The law of arms referred to two things: 1) Drawing a sword in the residence of the King was a mortal offense, and 2) For two soldiers in the English army to draw swords and fight each other in wartime was a mortal offense.

Basset continued, "But I'll go to his majesty, and request that I may have the liberty to avenge this wrong. When you shall see me next time, I'll meet you to your cost."

"Well, miscreant, I'll be there before the King as soon as you," Vernon said, "and after the King grants us permission to fight, I will meet you sooner than you wish."

CHAPTER 4

— 4.1 —

In a hall of state in Paris, the coronation of King Henry VI as King of France was being held. Present were King Henry VI, the Duke of Gloucester, the Bishop of Winchester, the Duke of York, the Earl of Suffolk, the Duke of Somerset, the Earl of Warwick, Lord Talbot, the Duke of Exeter, the Governor of Paris, and others.

The Duke of Gloucester said, "Lord Bishop of Winchester, set the crown upon his head."

The Bishop of Winchester set the crown on Henry VI's head and said, "God save King Henry, of that name the sixth!"

"Now, governor of Paris, take your oath," the Duke of Gloucester said. "Swear that you acknowledge no other King but him. Esteem as your friends none but such as are his friends, and esteem as your foes none but such as shall intend malicious intrigues against his state: Swear that this shall you do, so help you righteous God!"

Sir John Fastolfe entered the room and interrupted the ceremony, saying to King Henry VI, "My gracious sovereign, as I rode from Calais to hasten to your coronation, a letter was delivered to my hands. It was written to your grace by the Duke of Burgundy."

Lord Talbot recognized Sir John Fastolfe — the cowardly knight who had fled from battle earlier. Upset by that and by the interruption of the ceremony, he said, "Shame to the Duke of Burgundy and to you! I vowed, base knight, that when I next met you, I would tear the garter from your coward's leg."

Sir John Fastolfe was a member of the Order of the Garter, the highest order of knights. They wore a garter just below the left knee. Of course, Lord Talbot did not think that such a cowardly knight should be a member of the Order of the Garter.

Lord Talbot removed Sir John's garter and said, "Now I have done that because you were unworthily installed in that high degree.

"Pardon me, King Henry VI, and the rest of you. This coward, at the battle of Patay, when my army was in all only six thousand strong and we were outnumbered by the French almost ten to one, even before we met or a single stroke of the sword was given, like a 'trusty' contemptible fellow this man ran away. In that battle we lost twelve hundred men. I myself and several other gentlemen besides me were there surprised and taken prisoner.

"So then judge, great lords, if I have done anything amiss in tearing away this fellow's garter. Decide whether such cowards ought to wear this ornament of knighthood — yes or no."

The Duke of Gloucester said, "To say the truth, this fellow's deed was infamous and ill beseeming any common man; this deed is even more ill beseeming a knight, a Captain, and a leader."

Lord Talbot said, "When this order was first ordained, my lords, knights of the garter were of noble birth, valiant and virtuous, and full of high-minded courage. They were such as earned good reputations in the wars; they did not fear death, nor recoil because of distress, but instead they were always resolute in the direst situations.

"A man who lacks those honorable virtues yet calls himself a knight does nothing but usurp the sacred name of knight; he profanes this most honorable order of knighthood, and he should, if I were worthy enough to be his judge, be quite degraded, like a hedge-born swain who presumes to boast that he has noble blood."

A "hedge-born swain" is a peasant born under a hedge.

King Henry VI believed everything that Lord Talbot had said, so he said to Sir John Fastolfe, "Stain and disgrace to your countrymen, you hear your judgment! Be off, therefore, you who were a knight. From this time on we banish you, on pain of death."

Disgraced, John Fastolfe, who had previously been Sir John Fastolfe, exited.

King Henry VI then said, "And now, Duke of Gloucester, my Lord Protector, view the letter sent from our uncle the Duke of Burgundy."

One of King Henry VI's uncles was the Duke of Bedford, who had married Anne, the sister of the Duke of Burgundy, and so King Henry VI and the Duke of Burgundy were related by marriage.

The Duke of Gloucester first looked at how the letter was addressed. Normally it would acknowledge Henry VI as King of France as well as of England and Wales, and it would include an acknowledgement that Henry VI was the writer's sovereign.

The Duke of Gloucester said, "What does his grace mean, that he has changed his style? Nothing more but, plainly and bluntly, '*To the King*!' Has he forgotten that Henry VI is his sovereign? Or does this churlish address portend some alteration in good will?

"What's written here in the letter?"

He then read the letter out loud:

"I have, upon special cause, moved with compassion for my country's destruction, together with the pitiful complaints of such people as your oppression feeds upon, forsaken your pernicious faction and joined with Charles, the rightful King of France."

The Duke of Gloucester then said, "Oh, monstrous treachery! Can this be true? Can it be that in alliance, amity, and oaths, there should be found such false dissembling and deceitful guile?"

"What!" King Henry VI said. "Is my uncle Burgundy rebelling against me?"

"He is, my lord," the Duke of Gloucester said. "He has become your foe."

"Is that the worst of the news that this letter contains?" King Henry VI asked.

"It is the worst, and it is all, my lord, that he writes," the Duke of Gloucester replied.

"Why, then, Lord Talbot there shall talk with him and chastise him for this abuse," King Henry VI said.

He then asked Lord Talbot, "What do you say, my lord? Are you willing to do this?"

"Willing, my liege!" Lord Talbot said. "Yes, I am. If you had not already given me this duty, I would have begged you to give it to me."

King Henry VI ordered, "Then gather strength and march against him immediately. Let him perceive how ill we endure his treason and what an offence it is to flout and abuse his friends."

"I go now, my lord," Lord Talbot said. "In my heart I desire always that you may see the destruction of your foes."

Lord Talbot exited.

Vernon and Basset entered the room. Vernon was wearing a white rose, and Basset was wearing a red rose.

Vernon asked King Henry VI, "Grant me the right of combat, gracious sovereign. Grant me the right of trial by duel."

Basset said, "And, my lord, grant me the combat, too."

The Duke of York said about Vernon, "This is my retainer. Hear what he has to say, noble King."

The Duke of Somerset said about Basset, "And this is my retainer. Sweet Henry, show him favor. Give him what he wants."

"Be patient, lords," King Henry VI said, "and allow them to speak.

"Say, gentlemen, what makes you thus exclaim? And why do you crave combat? And with whom?"

Vernon pointed to Basset and said, "With him, my lord; for he has done me wrong."

Basset said about Vernon, "And I with him, for he has done me wrong."

"What is that wrong whereof you both complain?" King Henry VI said. "First let me know, and then I'll give you your answer to your request."

Basset said, "Crossing the sea from England into France, this fellow here, with a malicious, carping tongue, upbraided me about the red rose I wear, saying that the blood-red color of the leaves represented my master's blushing cheeks when my master stubbornly rejected the truth about a certain question in the law argued between the Duke of York and him. Vernon also used other vile and ignominious terms. In rebuttal of that rude and ignorant reproach and in defense of my lord's worthiness, I beg the benefit and legal privilege of fighting a duel."

"And that is also my petition, noble lord," Vernon said. "For although he seems with counterfeit and cunning ingenuity to give an attractive appearance to his bold intention, yet you should know, my lord, I was provoked by him, and he first took exceptions at this badge, this white rose, saying that the paleness of this flower revealed the faintness of my master's heart."

The Duke of York asked, "Won't this malice, Somerset, cease?"

The Duke of Somerset replied, "Your private grudge, my Lord of York, will out and be known, no matter how cunningly you try to cover it up."

King Henry VI said, "Good Lord, what madness rules in brainsick men, when for so slight and frivolous a cause such factious conflicts shall arise! York and Somerset, you are good kinsmen both to yourselves and to me, so quiet yourselves, please, and be at peace."

The Duke of York said, "Let this dissension first be tried by fight, and then your highness shall command a peace."

The Duke of Somerset said, "The quarrel concerns none but us alone. Between ourselves let us decide it then."

The Duke of York threw down his white rose and said, "There is my pledge; accept it, Somerset. Pick it up, and let's duel."

Vernon said, "Nay, let the fight rest where it began at first."

He meant that only Basset and he should fight; the Duke of York and the Duke of Somerset ought not to duel each other.

Basset said, "Confirm it so, my honorable lord. Let Vernon and I fight a duel."

"Confirm it so!" the Duke of Gloucester said. "Confounded be your strife! And may you two perish, with your audacious prattle! Presumptuous vassals, aren't you ashamed with this immodest clamorous outrage of yours to trouble and disturb the King and us?

"And you, my lords York and Somerset, I think you aren't doing well to allow them to make their perverse accusations, much less for you two to take the opportunity from their mouths to raise a civil disturbance between yourselves. Let me persuade you to take a better course of action."

The Duke of Exeter said, "This quarrel grieves his highness. My good lords, be friends."

King Henry VI said, "Come here, Vernon and Basset, you who would be combatants. From henceforth I order you, as you love our favor, entirely to forget this quarrel and its cause.

"And you, my lords York and Somerset, remember where we are. We are in France, in the midst of a fickle and wavering nation. If they perceive dissension in our looks and if they perceive that among ourselves we disagree, how will their resentful feelings be provoked to willful disobedience and rebellion!

"Besides, what infamy will there arise when foreign Princes shall be informed that for a toy, a thing of no regard, King Henry VI's peers and chief nobility have destroyed themselves and lost the realm of France!

"Think upon the conquest of my father and think upon my tender years, and let us not forego for a trifle that which was bought with blood. Let me be the umpire in this disquieting dispute."

He got a red rose, the emblem of the Lancastrians, and wore it and said, "I see no reason, if I wear this rose, that any one should therefore be suspicious I incline more to Somerset than to York. Both are my kinsmen, and I love them both. People may as well upbraid me for wearing my crown because, in fact, the King of Scots also wears a crown."

King Henry VI and the Duke of Somerset were both members of the House of Lancaster. Henry VI's father, Henry V, held the title of Duke of Lancaster. Once he became King Henry V, the title of Duke of Lancaster and his other titles became merged in the crown.

King Henry VI continued, "But your discretions can better persuade than I am able to instruct or teach. And therefore, as we came here in peace, so let us always continue to co-exist in peace and love.

"Kinsman of York, we appoint your grace to be our Regent in these parts of France.

"And, my good Lord of Somerset, unite your troops of horsemen with the Duke of York's bands of soldiers.

"York and Somerset, like true subjects, sons of your progenitors, go cheerfully together and expend your angry choler on your enemies.

"We ourself, my Lord Protector, and the rest of us after some respite will return to Calais. From thence we will go to England, where I hope before long to be presented, as a result of your victories, with Charles the Dauphin, the Duke of Alençon, and that traitorous rabble."

Everyone exited except for the Duke of York, the Earl of Warwick, the Duke of Exeter, and Vernon.

The Earl of Warwick said, "My Lord of York, I assure you I thought that the King prettily played the orator."

"And so he did," the Duke of York said, "but yet I don't like his wearing the badge — the red rose — of Somerset."

"Tush, that was but his fancy, so don't blame him; I dare presume, sweet Prince, that he thought no harm," the Earl of Warwick said.

"If I knew for sure that he did — but let it rest," the Duke of York said. "Other affairs must now be managed."

Everyone exited except for the Duke of Exeter, who said to himself, "You did well, Richard, the Duke of York, to suppress your voice and opinion because if the passions of your heart had burst out, I am afraid that we should have seen there more rancorous spite and more furious raging quarrels than yet can be imagined or supposed. Nevertheless, no common man who sees this jarring discord of nobility, this jostling of each other in the court, this partisan verbal strife of their supporters, can think other than that it presages some ill event.

"It is a serious matter when scepters are in children's hands, but it is a much more serious matter when malice breeds unnatural separation and division among members of the same family. When that happens, there comes the rain — there begins confusion and destruction."

A proverb stated, "Woe to the land whose King is a child."

Despite their hatred of each other, the Duke of York and the Duke of Somerset were both descended from King Edward III.

Lord Talbot, accompanied by a trumpeter and a drummer, stood outside the wall of the French city of Bordeaux and ordered, "Go to the gates of Bordeaux, trumpeter. Summon their General to the wall."

The trumpet sounded, and the French General and some others arrived and stood on the wall of the city.

Lord Talbot said, "English John Talbot, who is a servant in arms to Harry, King of England, calls you Captains forth, and this is what I want: Open your city gates, be humble to us, call my sovereign yours, and do him homage as obedient subjects. If you do these things, I'll withdraw both my bloodthirsty army and myself. But if you frown upon this proffered peace, then you tempt the fury of my three attendants — lean famine, quartering steel, and climbing fire — who in a moment shall lay your stately and air-defying towers level with the earth if you forsake the offer of their love."

"Quartering steel" referred to steel weapons that could dismember and quarter — cut into four pieces — bodies.

The French General replied, "You ominous and fearful owl of death, you who are our nation's terror and their bloody scourge! The end of your tyranny approaches."

In this culture, the screech of the owl was thought to prophesy death.

The French General continued, "You cannot enter into our city except by dying first, for I assure you, we are well fortified and are strong enough to issue out of the city and fight you. If you retreat from the city, Charles the Dauphin, who has a well-armed army, stands by with the snares of war to entangle you. On either side of you are squadrons who are ready for combat and who will wall you away from the liberty of flight. You can turn to no place for help. Every place you look you will find death in front of you with plainly evident slaughter, and pale destruction will meet you face to face. Ten thousand Frenchmen have taken the sacrament and sworn to make their dangerous artillery explode upon no Christian soul but English Talbot.

"Lo, there you stand, a breathing valiant man with an invincible and unconquered spirit! This is the latest and last glory of your praise that I, your enemy, will endow you with, for before the hourglass, which now begins to run, finishes the progression of its sandy hour, these eyes that see you now well colored and in ruddy good health shall see you withered, bloody, pale, and dead."

Drums sounded in the distance.

The French General continued, "Listen! Listen! The Dauphin's drum is a warning bell that sings heavy, serious music to your timorous soul, and my soul shall ring your dire departure — your horrible death — out."

The French General and the people with him exited from the wall.

Lord Talbot said, "He is not telling a fable; he is not lying. I hear the enemy's drums."

He ordered, "Go out, some lightly armed horsemen, and spy on their flanks."

He then said, "Oh, negligent, careless, and heedless military discipline! We are parked and bounded in a pale, an area bounded by a fence. We are like a little herd of England's timorous, fearful deer, amazed and bewildered by a yelping kennel of French curs!

"But if we be English deer, then let us be in blood. Let us be in full vigor and not like rascals — weak deer that will fall down after suffering a mere nip from a dog. Let us instead be moody-mad, furiously angry, and desperate stags. Let us turn on the bloody hounds with heads of steel — hard antlers, or steel weapons — and make the cowards stand aloof at bay."

The French would have Lord Talbot and his army at bay; Lord Talbot and his army would be like a deer making a last stand after being surrounded by hunting dogs. But Lord Talbot and his army would make the enemy stand aloof — stand back and be afraid to fight for a while, despite their advantage.

Lord Talbot continued, "If every Englishman sells his life as dearly as I intend to sell mine, then the Frenchmen shall find dear deer of us, my friends.

"By God and Saint George, Talbot, and England's right, may our battle flags prosper in this dangerous fight!"

On a plain in Gascony, a messenger met the Duke of York. With the Duke of York were a trumpeter and many soldiers.

The Duke of York asked, "Have the speedy scouts who dogged and tracked the mighty army of the Dauphin returned again?"

The messenger said, "They have returned, my lord, and they report that the Dauphin and his army have marched to Bordeaux to fight Lord Talbot. As the Dauphin and his army marched along, your spies saw two mightier armies than that the Dauphin led; these two armies joined with him and also marched for Bordeaux."

The Duke of York said, "May a plague fall upon that villain the Duke of Somerset, who thus delays my promised supply of horsemen who were levied for this siege! Renowned Talbot expects my aid, but I am treated with contempt by a traitor villain and cannot help the noble chevalier. May God comfort and help him in this difficulty! If he suffers death, farewell to wars in France."

Sir William Lucy arrived and said to the Duke of York, "You Princely leader of our English strength, never were you so needed on the soil of France. Spur to the rescue of the noble Talbot, who now is girdled with a waist of iron and hemmed about with grim destruction: A belt of enemy warriors encircles him. Go to Bordeaux, warlike Duke! Go to Bordeaux, York! If you do not, then farewell, Talbot, France, and England's honor."

The Duke of York said, "Oh, God, I wish that the Duke of Somerset, whose proud heart prevents the departure of my troops of cavalry and will not allow them to come to me, were in Talbot's place! If that were so, we would save a valiant gentleman — Lord Talbot — by forfeiting the Duke of Somerset, who is a traitor and a coward. Mad ire and wrathful fury make me weep because we die like this, while remiss, careless traitors sleep."

Sir William Lucy pleaded, "Oh, send some succor to the distressed lord!"

The Duke of York said, "He — Talbot — dies, and we lose; I break my warlike word — my word as a soldier. We mourn, and France smiles. We lose, but they daily gain. All of this happens because of this vile traitor Somerset."

Sir William Lucy said, "Then may God have mercy on brave Talbot's soul, and on young John, his son whom two hours ago I met as he traveled toward his warlike, valiant father! For the past seven years, Talbot has not seen his son, and now they meet where both their lives are done. They meet only to die together."

The Duke of York said, "Alas, what joy shall noble Talbot have to bid his young son welcome to his grave? Leave! Vexation and grief almost stop my breath, seeing that separated relatives should greet each other in the hour of death. Sir William Lucy, farewell; my fortune is that I can do no more than curse the reason — the Duke of Somerset — why I cannot aid the Talbot.

"Maine, Blois, Poictiers, and Tours are won away from England, all because of the Duke of Somerset and his delay in sending me my troops of cavalry."

The Duke of York and his trumpeter and soldiers exited.

Alone, Sir William Lucy said to himself, "Thus, while the vulture of sedition feeds in the bosom of such great commanders, sleeping neglect betrays to loss the conquest of our scarcely cold conqueror of France, that man who forever lives in our memory: Henry V. While the Duke of York and the Duke of Somerset thwart and cross each other, lives, honors, lands, and all hurry to loss."

On another plain in Gascony was the Earl of Somerset's army. The Earl of Somerset talked with one of Lord Talbot's Captains.

The Earl of Somerset said, "It is too late; I cannot send them now. The Duke of York and Lord Talbot too rashly planned this expedition. Our whole army might be engaged and fought with in a sudden attack by the town's own garrison. The over-daring Talbot has sullied all his gloss of former honor by this heedless, desperate, wild adventure. The Duke of York set him on to fight and die in shame, so that once Talbot is dead, the Duke of York might bear a greater name."

The Captain looked up and said, "Here comes Sir William Lucy, who with me set forth from our overmatched forces for aid."

"How are you now, Sir William!" the Earl of Somerset asked. "Whither were you sent?"

"Whither" means "to which place." Sir William Lucy had been sent to the Duke of York, but he did not want to mention that because it was off-topic. Sir William Lucy had more important things to say. He realized that any reinforcements would arrive after the battle. But he wanted to test the Duke of Somerset and see if he would agree immediately to send reinforcements, and especially if he would not, Sir William Lucy wanted the Duke of Somerset to know the consequences of his actions. The Duke of Somerset should have already sent reinforcements; he should have sent them immediately when the Captain who had arrived before Sir William Lucy had asked for them.

"Whither, my lord?" he said. "I have come from Lord Talbot, who has been bought and sold and betrayed. He, ringed about with bold adversity, cries out for reinforcements from noble York and Somerset, to beat assailing death away from his weak legions, and while the honorable Captain Talbot there drops bloody sweat from his war-wearied limbs, and uses an advantageous military position to draw out and continue the battle while looking for rescue, you, his false hopes, the trust of England's honor, stay away, aloof with worthless rivalry.

"Don't allow your private discord to keep away the mustered reinforcements who should lend him aid, while he, a renowned noble gentleman, yields his life while fighting against immense odds. Orleans the

Bastard, Charles the Dauphin, the Duke of Burgundy, the Duke of Alençon, and Reignier surround him, and Talbot perishes because of your failure to do your duty."

"York set him on," the Duke of Somerset said. "York should have sent him aid."

"And York as quickly blames your grace, swearing that you are withholding his levied cavalry who were mustered for this expedition."

"York lies," the Duke of Somerset said. "He might have sent a request to me and had the cavalry. I owe him little duty, and less love. I think that it would be a foul disgrace to fawn on him by sending the cavalry to him without him first asking for them."

He was ignoring the earlier words of King Henry VI: "And, my good Lord of Somerset, unite your troops of horsemen with the Duke of York's bands of soldiers."

Sir William Lucy said, "The faithlessness of England, not the military might of France, has now entrapped the noble-minded Talbot. Never to England shall he bear his life; instead, he dies, betrayed to fortune by your strife."

"Come, let's go," the Earl of Somerset said. "I will dispatch the horsemen immediately. Within six hours they will be at his aid."

Sir William Lucy said, "Too late comes the rescue. He is either captured or slain. He could not flee and escape even if he wanted to, if it were possible for him to flee, and Talbot would never flee and escape, even if it were possible."

"If he is dead, then brave Talbot, adieu!" the Earl of Somerset said.

"His fame lives on in the world, but the shame of his death lives on in you," Sir William Lucy said.

Lord Talbot and John, his son, talked together in the English camp near Bordeaux.

Lord Talbot said, "Oh, young John Talbot! I sent for you so I could tutor you in the strategy of war, so that the name of Talbot might be revived in you when sapless, feeble old age and weak, incapable limbs would bring your drooping father to his chair in his retirement.

"But, oh, malignant and ill-boding stars! Now, my son, you have come to a feast of death, a terrible and unavoidable danger. Therefore, dear boy, mount my swiftest horse, and I'll direct you how you can escape by sudden flight. Come, don't dally, be gone and leave immediately."

John Talbot asked, "Is my name Talbot? And am I your son? And shall I flee? Oh, if you love my mother, don't dishonor her honorable name by making a bastard and a slave of me! The world will say, 'He is not Talbot's blood, not if he basely fled when noble Talbot stood his ground.'"

"Flee, so you can revenge my death, if I am slain," Lord Talbot said.

"He who flees so will never return again," John Talbot said. "He who flees once will continue to flee."

"If we both stay, we both are sure to die," Lord Talbot said.

"Then let me stay; and, father, you flee," John Talbot said. "If you die, the loss to our country will be great, so your regard for your life should be great. My worth is unknown, and if I die, our country will feel no loss. If I die, the French can little boast about it. If you die, the French will greatly boast. If you die, our country's hopes are all lost. Flight cannot stain the honor you have won, but if I flee, flight will stain my honor; I have done no noble exploits, and flight is all I will be remembered for. If you flee, everyone will swear that you made a strategic retreat for military advantage. But if I flee, they'll say it was out of fear. There is no hope that I ever will stay and fight, if in the first hour of battle I shrink and run away."

He knelt and said, "Here on my knee I beg mortality, rather than life preserved with infamy."

"Shall all your mother's hopes lie in one tomb?" Lord Talbot asked. "Shall her husband and her progeny all lie in one tomb, with no one left alive?"

"Yes, for that is preferable to my shaming my mother's womb," John Talbot replied.

"After I give you my blessing, I command you to go," Lord Talbot said.

"I will go to fight, but not to flee the foe," John Talbot said.

"Part of your father may be saved in you," Lord Talbot said. "If you stay alive, some part of me will continue to live."

"No part of you, my father, but only shame will be in me."

"You have never had renown, and therefore you cannot lose it."

"I have your renowned name: the name of Talbot. Shall flight dishonor and abuse it?" John Talbot said.

"Your father's order to you to flee shall clear you from that stain."

"You cannot be a witness for me, once you are slain. If death is so unavoidable and so apparent, then both of us should flee."

"And leave my followers here to fight and die?" Lord Talbot said. "My life has never been tainted with such shame."

"And shall my youth be guilty of such blame?" John Talbot said. "No more can I be severed from your side than you can divide yourself in two. Stay, go, do whatever you want to; whatever you decide to do, I will do it, also. I will not live, if my father dies."

"Then here I take my leave of you, fair son, you were born to eclipse and extinguish your life this afternoon."

He helped his son rise from the ground and added, "Come, side by side together we will live and die. And soul with soul from France to Heaven we will fly."

The battle started, and the English fought bravely. At one point, the Frenchmen came close to killing John Talbot, but Lord Talbot rescued him.

"Saint George and victory!" Lord Talbot shouted. "Fight, soldiers, fight! The Regent of France — the Duke of York — has broken his word to me, Lord Talbot, and left us to the rage of France's swordsmen.

"Where is John Talbot?"

Seeing him, he said, "Pause, and take your breath; I gave you life, and I rescued you from death."

"Oh, twice my father, twice am I your son!" John Talbot said. "The life you gave me first was lost and done, until with your warlike sword, in spite of fate, to my allotted time of life you gave me a new, later date to die."

Lord Talbot said, "When from the Dauphin's crest on his helmet your sword struck fire, it warmed your father's heart with proud desire of bold-faced victory. Then I, despite my leaden age, quickened with youthful spirits and warlike rage, beat down the Duke of Alençon, the Bastard of Orleans, and the Duke of Burgundy, and from the pride — the best soldiers — of Gallia, aka France, rescued you.

"The angry Bastard of Orleans, who drew blood from you, my boy, and had the maidenhood — the first blood — of your first fight, I soon encountered, and exchanging blows with him I quickly shed some of his bastard blood, and insultingly said to him, 'I am spilling your contaminated, base, and misbegotten blood, which is mean, ignoble, and very poor, for that pure blood of mine that you forced from Talbot, my brave boy.' Then, as I moved to destroy the Bastard and end his life, strong reinforcements came in to rescue him.

"Speak, your father's care and concern. Aren't you weary, John? How do you fare? Will you now leave the battle, boy, and flee, now that you are sealed and confirmed to be the son of chivalry?

"Flee in order to revenge my death when I am dead. The help of one person stands me in little stead — one person can help me very little. Too much folly is it, well I know, to hazard all our lives in one small boat!

"If I don't die today from the Frenchmen's rage, tomorrow I shall die with great old age. The Frenchmen gain nothing by my death if I stay: It is only the shortening of my life by one day. If you die, your mother dies, as does our household's name, my death's revenge, your youth, and England's fame. All these and more we hazard by your stay; all these are saved if you will flee away."

John Talbot replied, "The sword of the Bastard of Orleans has not made me smart, but these words of yours draw life-blood from my heart. To gain those benefits, bought with such a shame, would save a paltry life and slay bright fame. Before young Talbot from old Talbot flees, may the coward horse that bears me fall and die! And compare me to the peasant boys of France, to be shame's scorn and subject of mischance! Surely, by all the glory you have won, if I flee, I am not Talbot's son. So then, talk no more of flight, it does no good. If I am Talbot's son, I will die at Talbot's foot."

Lord Talbot said, "Then follow your desperate sire of Crete, you Icarus."

Icarus was the son of Daedalus, who designed the labyrinth at Crete to house the Minotaur, the half-bull, half-human man-eating monster. After Daedalus and his son were imprisoned on the island of Crete, Daedalus designed wings made of feathers and wax so that he and his son could fly over the sea to freedom. The wings worked, but Icarus flew too close to the Sun, the heat of which melted the wax, causing the feathers to molt. Icarus fell into the sea and drowned. Icarus could have lived, but his exuberance caused his death.

Lord Talbot continued, "Your life to me is sweet. If you must fight, then fight by your father's side, and now that you have proven yourself to be commendable, let's die proudly and with honor."

The battle continued. A servant helped Lord Talbot, exhausted by age and combat, to walk.

Lord Talbot asked, "Where is my other life? My own life is gone. Where's young Talbot? Where is valiant John? Triumphant Death, smeared with the blood of slain captives, young Talbot's valor makes me smile at you. When young Talbot saw me shrink down on my knee, he brandished his bloody sword over me, and like a hungry lion, he began to perform rough deeds of rage and stern impatience. But when my angry guard stood alone, tending to my ruin and assailed by none, dizzy-eyed fury and great rage of heart suddenly made him run from my side into the clustering battle of the French, and in that sea of blood my boy drenched his mounting-too-high spirit, and there died my Icarus, my blossom, in his pride."

The servant said, "My dear lord, look, your son is being borne here!"

Some soldiers arrived, carrying the corpse of John Talbot.

Lord Talbot said, "You grinning jester Death, who laughs at and scorns us here, soon, away from your insulting tyranny, coupled in bonds of perpetuity, two Talbots, winging through the yielding sky, shall spite you and escape mortality."

He then said to his son's corpse, "Oh, you, whose honorable wounds make handsome even the appearance of ugly death, speak to your father before you yield your breath! Defy death by speaking, whether or not he will allow you to speak. Imagine that Death is a Frenchman and your foe.

"Poor boy! He smiles, I think, as one who would say, 'Had Death been French, then Death would have died today.'"

He then ordered, "Come, come and lay him in his father's arms. My spirit can no longer bear these harms."

The soldiers brought John Talbot's corpse over to Lord Talbot, who hugged it and said, "Soldiers, adieu! I have what I want, now that my old arms are young John Talbot's grave."

Lord Talbot died.

Fighting broke out, and the servant and soldiers exited, leaving the two corpses behind.

After the battle was over and the French had won, Charles the Dauphin, the Duke of Alençon, the Duke of Burgundy, the Bastard of Orleans, Joan la Pucelle, and some soldiers entered the scene.

Charles the Dauphin said, "If the Duke of York and the Duke of Somerset had brought in reinforcements for the English, this would have been a bloody day for us."

The Bastard of Orleans marveled, "How the young whelp of Talbot's, raging-mad, fleshed his puny sword in Frenchmen's blood!"

He referred to John Talbot's sword as "puny" because its wielder had been untested in battle before this day.

Joan la Pucelle said, "Once I encountered him, and I said to him, 'You maiden — virgin — youth, be vanquished by a maiden.' But, with a proud and majestically high scorn, he answered, 'Young Talbot was not born to be the pillage of a giglot — a harlot — wench.' Then, rushing into the midst of the French, he left me proudly, considering me unworthy for him to fight."

The Duke of Burgundy said, "Doubtless he would have made a noble knight. Look at him. On the ground he lies, as if in a coffin, in the arms of the most bloodthirsty nurser of his harms!"

He felt that Lord Talbot had nursed — encouraged — his son to inflict wounds. In doing so, Lord Talbot had also made it possible for his son to suffer wounds.

The Bastard of Orleans said, "Hew them to pieces, hack their bones asunder. Their life was England's glory, and Gallia's wonder — France's object of astonishment."

Charles the Dauphin said, "No! Don't! Those whom during their life we have fled, let us not wrong them once they are dead."

Sir William Lucy arrived with some attendants. Walking in front of him was a French herald.

Sir William Lucy, who had arrived too late to participate in the battle, said, "Herald, conduct me to the Dauphin's tent, so I can learn who has obtained the glory of the day."

"On what submissive message have you been sent?" Charles the Dauphin asked. He expected Sir William Lucy to be carrying a message that what was left of the English army was surrendering to him.

"Submission, Dauphin!" Sir William Lucy said. "It is entirely a French word; we English warriors don't know what it means."

Sir William Lucy was aware that the English army had lost, but he was putting up a bold and brave front as he sought to learn the fate of Lord Talbot.

He added, "I have come to learn what prisoners you have taken and to survey the bodies of the dead."

"You ask about prisoners?" Charles the Dauphin said. "Our prison is Hell. We kill our prisoners. But tell me whom you seek."

Sir William Lucy asked, "Where's the great Alcides — Hercules — of the battlefield, valiant Lord Talbot, Earl of Shrewsbury, who was given many titles as a reward for his rare success in arms? He is the great Earl of Washford, Waterford, and Valence. He is Lord Talbot of Goodrig and Urchinfield, Lord Strange of Blackmere, Lord Verdun of Alton, Lord Cromwell of Wingfield, Lord Furnival of Sheffield, the thrice-victorious Lord of Falconbridge; knight of the noble order of Saint George, a worthy of Saint Michael and the Golden Fleece. He is also the great commander-in-chief to King Henry VI in all his wars within the realm of France. Where is he?"

"Here is a silly stately style indeed!" Joan la Pucelle said, mocking the list of titles. "The Sultan of Turkey, who has fifty-two Kingdoms, does not write as tedious a style as this. He whom you magnify with all these titles lies stinking and fly-blown here at our feet."

Already flies were buzzing around Lord Talbot's corpse.

Sir William Lucy said, "Has Lord Talbot been slain, the Frenchmen's only scourge, your kingdom's terror and black Nemesis?"

Nemesis was an ancient goddess who punished humans who were guilty of pride and arrogance against the gods.

Sir William Lucy continued, "I wish that my eyeballs would turn into bullets so that I in rage might shoot them at your faces! I wish that I could call these dead English warriors to life! It would be enough to frighten the realm of France. Even if only Lord Talbot's picture were left among you here, it would terrify the proudest of you all. Give me their bodies, so that I may bear them away from here and give them burial as befits their worth."

Joan la Pucelle said, "I think this upstart is old Talbot's ghost — he must be because he speaks with such a proud commanding spirit. For God's sake let him have the bodies; if we kept them here, they would only stink and putrefy the air."

Charles the Dauphin said, "Go and take their bodies away from here."

"I'll bear them away," Sir William Lucy said, "but from their ashes shall be reared a phoenix that shall make all France afraid."

In the Arden Shakespeare edition of *King Henry VI, Part 1*, editor Edward Burns writes, "According to myth there is only ever one phoenix bird at any one time, but it regenerates itself from the ashes of its funeral pyre, in the deserts of Arabia, so it is an emblem of the survival of individual worth in defiance of the logic of natural survival."

Charles the Dauphin replied, "As long as we are rid of them, do with them what you will."

He then said to the others, "And now to Paris, in this conquering vein. All will be ours, now bloodthirsty Talbot's slain."

CHAPTER 5

— 5.1 —

In the palace in London, King Henry VI was meeting with the Duke of Gloucester and the Duke of Exeter.

He asked the Duke of Gloucester, "Have you perused the letters from the Pope, the Holy Roman Emperor, and the Earl of Armagnac?"

"I have, my lord," the Duke of Gloucester replied, "and their purpose is this: They humbly petition your excellence to have a godly peace brought into existence between the realms of England and of France."

"How does your grace like their proposal?"

"I like it well, my good lord, and I think it is the only way to stop the spilling of our Christian blood and establish peace on every side."

"Yes, that is true, by the Virgin Mary, uncle," King Henry VI said, "for I always thought it was both impious and unnatural that such inhuman, atrocious savagery and bloody strife should reign among professors of one faith. The English and the French are Christian."

"In addition, my lord, the sooner to effect and the surer to bind this knot of amity, the Earl of Armagnac, who is closely related to Charles the Dauphin and who is a man of great authority in France, offers his only daughter to your grace in marriage, along with a large and sumptuous dowry. This is a marriage that will advance peace between England and France."

"Marriage, uncle!" King Henry VI said. "Alas, my years are young! And it is more suitable for me to devote myself to my study and my books than to engage in wanton dalliance with a paramour.

"Yet call the ambassadors, and as you please, let every one of them have their answers. I shall be well content with any choice that tends to God's glory and my country's well-being."

The Bishop of Winchester had officially become the Cardinal of Winchester. Dressed in the clothing of a Cardinal, he entered the room, along with the three ambassadors representing the Pope, the Holy Roman Emperor, and the Earl of Armagnac. The ambassador representing the Pope was a Papal Legate.

Seeing the Cardinal of Winchester, the Duke of Exeter said to himself, "Has my Lord of Winchester been officially installed as a Cardinal and been given a Cardinal's rank? Then I perceive that what King Henry V once prophesied will be verified as true: 'If once Winchester comes to be a Cardinal, he'll make his Cardinal's cap equal to the crown.'"

King Henry VI said, "My lords ambassadors, your several petitions have been considered and debated. And therefore we are for certain resolved to draft the conditions of a friendly peace, which we intend shall be transported immediately to France by my Lord of Winchester."

The Duke of Gloucester said to the ambassador of the Earl of Armagnac, "And as for the offer to my lord from your master, I have informed at length his highness of it, and as he likes the lady's virtuous gifts, her beauty, and the value of her dowry, he intends that she shall be his wife and the Queen of England."

King Henry VI said, "As evidence and proof of this marriage contract, take to her and give her this jewel as a pledge of my affection, and so, my Lord Protector, see them safeguarded and safely brought to Dover, where after they board a ship, commit them to the fortune of the sea."

Everyone exited except for the Cardinal of Winchester and the Papal Legate.

"Wait, my lord Legate," the Cardinal of Winchester said. "You shall first receive the sum of money that I promised would be delivered to his holiness for clothing me in these grave ornaments — this habit of a Cardinal."

"I will attend upon your lordship's leisure," the Papal Legate said. "I am ready when you are ready."

The Cardinal of Winchester said to himself, "Now I, Winchester, will not submit, I think, or be inferior to the proudest peer. Duke of Gloucester, you shall well perceive that, neither in birth nor in authority, I the Bishop will be put down or overruled by you. I'll either make you stoop and bend your knee to me, or sack this country with a mutinous rebellion."

Although he had become a Cardinal, he had not ceased being a Bishop.

— 5.2 —

On the plains of Anjou, France, Charles the Dauphin was meeting with the Duke of Burgundy, the Duke of Alençon, the Bastard of Orleans, Reignier, and Joan la Pucelle. Soldiers were present. Charles the Dauphin held a letter in his hand.

Charles the Dauphin said, "This news, my lords, may cheer our drooping spirits. It is said that the brave Parisians are revolting against the English and are turning again into the warlike French."

The Duke of Alençon said, "Then march to Paris, royal Charles of France, and don't keep back your armies in dalliance."

Joan la Pucelle said, "May peace be among the Parisians, if they turn to us and join us; otherwise, let devastation battle against their palaces!"

A scout arrived and said, "Success to our valiant General, and happiness to his accomplices!"

"What news do our scouts send?" Charles the Dauphin said. "Please, speak."

The scout said, "The English army, which was divided into two parties, is now joined into one, and it intends to fight you soon."

"Somewhat too sudden, sirs, the warning is," Charles the Dauphin said, "but we will soon provide for them."

The Duke of Burgundy said, "I trust that the ghost of Lord Talbot is not there. Now that he is gone, my lord, you need not fear."

"Of all base passions, fear is the most accursed," Joan la Pucelle said. "Command the conquest, Charles, it shall be yours. Let Henry VI fret and all the world complain."

She sounded positive that the French would defeat the English.

"Then let's go on, my lords," Charles the Dauphin said, "and may France be fortunate!"

The battle was taking place before Angiers.

Joan la Pucelle, alone, said, "The Regent — the English Duke of York — conquers, and the Frenchmen flee. Now help, you magic spells and amulets and you excellent spirits who forewarn me and give me signs of future events."

Thunder sounded as the fiends came closer.

Joan la Pucelle said, "You speedy helpers, who are subordinates of the lordly monarch of the north, appear and aid me in this enterprise."

Lucifer is "the lordly monarch of the north," according to Isaiah 14:12-14 (King James Version):

12 How art thou fallen from heaven, O Lucifer, son of the morning! how art thou cut down to the ground, which didst weaken the nations!

13 For thou hast said in thine heart, I will ascend into heaven, I will exalt my throne above the stars of God: I will sit also upon the mount of the congregation, in the sides of the north:

14 I will ascend above the heights of the clouds; I will be like the most High."

The fiends arrived.

Joan la Pucelle said, "This speedy and quick appearance argues proof of your accustomed diligence to me. You have always served me well. Now, you familiar spirits, who are culled out of the powerful regions under the earth, help me this once so that France may gain control of the battlefield."

The fiends walked around; they did not speak to Joan la Pucelle.

She said, "Oh, don't hold me here with your silence very long! I used to be accustomed to feed you with my blood, but now I'll lop a limb off and give it to you as a down payment of a further benefit — if you condescend to help me now."

In this culture, witches were thought to have an extra nipple that they used to feed the witches' human blood to attendant fiends.

The fiends hung their heads.

Joan la Pucelle said, "I have no hope to have help? My body shall pay the recompense, if you will grant my request for help."

The fiends shook their heads.

She said, "Can't my body or my blood-sacrifice persuade you to give me your usual help? Then take my soul, my body, soul and all, before England defeats the French."

The fiends exited.

She said, "See, they forsake me! Now the time has come that France must cast down her lofty-plumed crest and let her head fall into England's lap. My ancient incantations are too weak, and Hell is too strong for me to fight. Now, France, your glory droops to the dust."

The battle continued.

The Duke of York and the Duke of Burgundy fought, the French fled, and the Duke of York took Joan la Pucelle captive.

The Duke of York said, "Damsel of France, I think I have you fast. Unchain your spirits now with incantatory charms and see if they can gain for you your liberty. You are a splendid prize, fit for the Devil's respect! Look at how the ugly wench bends her brows and frowns, as if like Circe she would change my shape!"

Circe is an enchantress who in Homer's *Odyssey* changes Odysseus' men into swine.

"Changed into a worse shape you cannot be," Joan la Pucelle said.

"Charles the Dauphin is a proper man," the Duke of York said. "No shape but his can please your dainty eye."

"May a plaguing misfortune light both on Charles and on you!" Joan la Pucelle said. "And may both of you be suddenly surprised by bloody hands as you lie sleeping in your beds!"

"Cruel, cursing hag, enchantress, hold your tongue!" the Duke of York said.

"I ask you to give me permission to curse for awhile," Joan la Pucelle said.

"Curse, miscreant, when you are tied to the stake and burned," the Duke of York said.

He dragged her away.

The battle continued, and the Earl of Suffolk, aka William de la Pole, captured Margaret, the daughter of Reignier, and held her by the hand.

"Whoever you are, you are my prisoner," he said.

Looking at her, he said, "Oh, fairest beauty, do not fear or flee, for I will touch you only with reverent hands. I kiss these my fingers as a pledge of eternal peace, and lay them gently on your tender cheek. Who are you? Tell me, so that I may honor you."

She replied, "Margaret is my name, and I am daughter to a King — the King of Naples — whoever you are."

"I am an Earl, and I am called Suffolk," he said. "Don't be offended, nature's miracle, you were destined to be captured by me. So does the swan her downy cygnets — her offspring — protect, keeping them prisoner underneath her wings. Yet, if this servile usage should offend you, go and be free again, as Suffolk's friend."

She began to leave.

"Wait!" he said. "Stay here! I have no power to let her leave. My hand would free her, but my heart says no. Just like the sunshine plays upon the smooth, mirrory streams, twinkling another counterfeited, reflected, mirrored beam, so seems this gorgeous beauty to my eyes. She is as beautiful as sunshine gleaming on a smooth stream of water. I would like to woo her, yet I dare not speak. I'll call for pen and ink, and write my mind.

"Stop, de la Pole! Don't disparage yourself! Don't you have a tongue? Isn't she here in front of you? Will the sight of a woman daunt you?

"Yes, beauty's Princely majesty is such that it confuses the tongue and makes the senses rough."

Margaret said, "Tell me, Earl of Suffolk — if that is your name — what ransom must I pay before I can leave? For I perceive that I am your prisoner."

The Earl of Suffolk said to himself, "How can you know that she will deny my wooing of her, before you make a trial of her love?"

Margaret said, "Why don't you speak? What ransom must I pay?"

The Earl of Suffolk said to himself, "She is beautiful, and therefore to be wooed. She is a woman, and therefore to be won."

Margaret said, "Will you accept a ransom? Yes, or no?"

The Earl of Suffolk said to himself, "Foolish man, remember that you have a wife. How then can Margaret be your paramour?"

Margaret said to herself, "It is best for me to leave him, for he will not hear what I say to him."

The Earl of Suffolk said to himself, "There all is marred; there lies a cooling card."

A cooling card is something that cools all your hopes.

Margaret said to herself, "He talks at random; surely, the man is mad."

The Earl of Suffolk said to himself, "And yet a dispensation may be had."

The dispensation he meant was an annulment of his marriage.

Margaret said to herself, "And yet I wish that you would answer me."

The Earl of Suffolk said to himself, "I'll win this Lady Margaret. For whom? Why, for my King! Tush, that's a wooden thing!"

The wooden — stupid and insane — thing was the action of winning Margaret for someone other than himself.

Margaret said to herself, "He talks of wood. He is some carpenter."

The Earl of Suffolk said to himself, "Yet even so my fancy for her may be satisfied, and peace can be established between these realms. But there remains a difficulty in that, too, for although her father is the King of Naples, as well as the Duke of Anjou and Maine, yet he is poor, and our English nobles will scorn the match. She can bring King Henry VI no dowry."

"Can you hear me, Captain?" Margaret asked. "Aren't you at leisure? Don't you have time to speak to me?"

She was angry, and so she called him by the lower military title "Captain" rather than the higher noble title "Earl."

The Earl of Suffolk said to himself, "A marriage between King Henry VI and Margaret shall take place, no matter how much our English nobles disdain it. Henry is young and will quickly agree to the marriage."

He then said to Margaret, "Madam, I have a secret to reveal."

Margaret ignored him and said to herself, "What though I am a captive? He seems to be a knight, and he will not in any way dishonor me."

The Earl of Suffolk said, "Lady, please listen to what I have to say."

Margaret ignored him and said to herself, "Perhaps the French shall rescue me, and then I need not beg his courtesy."

The Earl of Suffolk said, "Sweet madam, give me a hearing in a cause —"

Margaret ignored him and said to herself, "Tush, women have been made captives before now."

The Earl of Suffolk said, "Lady, why do you talk so?"

"I beg your pardon," Margaret said, "but it is Quid for Quo. You ignored me as I tried to talk to you, and so now I ignored you as you tried to talk to me."

"Tell me, gentle Princess, would you not suppose that your bondage is happy, if you were to be made a Queen?"

Margaret replied, "To be a Queen in bondage is more vile than to be a slave in base servility, for Princes, Princesses, and nobles should be free."

"And so shall you, if happy England's royal King is free."

Was King Henry VI free? Or was he in bondage to the many people who wanted to manipulate him?

"Why, what concern is his freedom to me?" Margaret asked. "What does his freedom have to do with me?"

"I'll undertake to make you King Henry VI's Queen, put a golden scepter in your hand, and set a precious crown upon your head, if you will agree to be my —"

He paused.

Margaret asked, "What?"

The Earl of Suffolk said, "*His* love."

Margaret replied, "I am unworthy to be King Henry VI's wife."

"No, gentle madam; I am unworthy to woo so fair a dame to be his wife and have no portion in the choice myself."

"The choice" is the thing chosen, aka Margaret. The Earl of Suffolk felt that he was worthy of having a share of Margaret; to woo her and *not* have a share of her was beneath him.

He added, "What do you say, madam? Does this content you? Are you happy with what I have said?"

"If it pleases my father, then it pleases me."

"Then let's call our Captains and our battle flags forth. And, madam, at your father's castle wall we'll crave a parley, so we can confer with him."

A parley sounded. Reignier appeared on the castle wall.

The Earl of Suffolk said, "Look, Reignier, look, your daughter has been taken prisoner!"

"To whom is she prisoner?" Reignier asked.

"To me," the Earl of Suffolk replied.

"Earl of Suffolk, why do you tell me this? I am a soldier, and I am not suited to weep or to complain about Lady Fortune's fickleness."

"There is a remedy for this situation your daughter is in, my lord," the Earl of Suffolk said. "Consent, and for your honor give consent, that your daughter shall be wedded to my King. You will benefit from the marriage. Your daughter

I have taken pains to woo, and I have won her for King Henry VI. And this her easily endured imprisonment has gained your daughter Princely liberty."

"Is the Earl of Suffolk saying what he really thinks to be the truth?" Reignier asked.

If Margaret were to marry King Henry VI of England, she would be marrying out of her league.

The Earl of Suffolk replied, "Fair Margaret knows that I, the Earl of Suffolk, do not flatter, make a false face, or feign."

"Upon your noble guarantee of my safety, I will descend to give you the answer to your just question," Reignier said.

The Earl of Suffolk nodded to assure Reignier that he would be safe, and he said, "Here I will await your coming."

Reignier came down from his castle wall.

Reignier said, "Welcome, brave Earl of Suffolk, into our territories. Command in Anjou whatever your honor pleases."

"I thank you, Reignier. You are happy and fortunate to have so sweet a child, a child suitable to be made marital companion to a King. What answer does your grace make to my petition?"

"Since you deign to woo her little worth to be the Princely bride of such a lord, my daughter shall be Henry VI's, if he wants her, on the condition that I may quietly enjoy what is my own, the territories of Maine and Anjou, free from oppression or the stroke of war."

From the English perspective, the territories of Maine and Anjou actually belonged to England, not to Reignier.

"That is her ransom," the Earl of Suffolk said. "I release her to you, and I will make sure that your grace shall well and quietly enjoy those two territories."

"And in Henry VI's royal name, I again give her hand to you, who are acting as that gracious King's deputy. This action is a sign of plighted faith, a sign that the two are engaged to be married."

The Earl of Suffolk replied, "Reignier of France, I give you Kingly thanks because this business has been performed for a King."

He thought, *And yet, I think, I could be well content to be my own attorney in this case; I would like to woo Margaret for myself and make her mine.*

He said, "I'll go over then to England with this news, and make this marriage solemnized. So farewell, Reignier. Set this diamond — your daughter — safe in golden palaces that are suitable for it."

"I embrace you, as I would embrace the Christian Prince, King Henry VI, if he were here," Reignier said.

Margaret said to the Earl of Suffolk, "Farewell, my lord. You, Earl of Suffolk, shall always have good wishes, praise, and prayers from me, Margaret."

Reignier left, and Margaret started to go after him, but the Earl of Suffolk said, "Farewell, sweet madam, but listen, Margaret, have you no noble greetings for my King?"

"Tell him such greetings from me as are suitable for a maiden, a virgin, and his servant to say to him."

"These are words sweetly placed and modestly directed," the Earl of Suffolk said, "But madam, I must trouble you again. Have you no loving token for his majesty?"

"Yes, my good lord, I send to the King a pure unspotted heart, never yet affected by love."

"Also send him this," the Earl of Suffolk said, kissing her.

"That you yourself can send him," Margaret said. "I will not be so presumptuous as to send such peevish, silly, foolish tokens to a King."

Margaret exited.

The Earl of Suffolk said to himself, "Oh, I wish that you were mine! But, Suffolk, stop. You must not wander in that labyrinth; there Minotaurs and ugly treasons lurk."

The labyrinth was where the mythological Minotaur of Crete was kept. The Cretan Princess Pasiphaë had sex with a bull and gave birth to the half-human, half-bull monster known as the Minotaur. Such sex was illicit, and the Earl of Suffolk, attracted as he was to Margaret, knew that sex with her would be illicit, and since she would be married to King Henry VI, his having an affair with her could be regarded as treason.

He continued, "This is what I will do: Solicit Henry with praise of her wonders. Think about her virtues that outshine the virtues of others. Think about her natural graces that eclipse art. Remember the image of these good qualities of hers often on the seas. I will do all these things so that, when I come to kneel at Henry VI's feet, I may dispossess him of his wits as he is astonished with wonder at Margaret."

99

At the military camp of the Duke of York at Anjou, the Duke of York and the Earl of Warwick talked. Others were present.

The Duke of York said, "Bring forth that sorceress who is condemned to burn at the stake."

Some guards brought Joan la Pucelle to him. A shepherd also came.

The shepherd said, "Ah, Joan, this kills your father's heart outright! I have sought you in every region far and near, and now that it is my fortune to find you, must I behold your untimely and cruel death? Ah, Joan, sweet daughter Joan, I'll die with you!"

Joan la Pucelle said, "Decrepit and miserable creature! Base, lowly born, ignoble wretch! I am descended from a nobler blood. You are no father and no friend of mine."

"No! No!" the shepherd said. "My lords, if it pleases you, what she says is not true. I did beget her, as all in the parish know. Her mother is still alive, and she can testify that Joan was the first fruit of my bachelorship."

In this culture, the word "bachelorship" had two meanings: 1) apprenticeship, and 2) time as a bachelor, aka unmarried man.

The Earl of Warwick said to Joan la Pucelle, "You are without grace. Will you deny your parentage? Will you reject your own father?"

The Duke of York said, "This argues what her kind of life has been. It has been wicked and vile; and so her death concludes her life."

"Don't, Joan," the shepherd said. "Why will you be so stubborn! God knows you are a piece of my flesh, and for your sake I have shed many a tear. Don't deny that I am your father, I request, gentle Joan."

"Peasant, avaunt!" Joan la Pucelle said. "Leave! Get lost!"

She then said to the Duke of York, "You have bribed this man for the purpose of obscuring my noble birth."

Prisoners of noble birth were treated better than other prisoners; often, they would be ransomed and allowed to live.

The shepherd said, "It is true that I gave a noble — a coin — to the priest the morning that I was wedded to her mother.

"Kneel down and take my blessing, my good girl. Will you not stoop for my blessing? Now cursed be the time of your nativity! I wish that the milk your mother gave you when you sucked her breast had been a little rat poison for your sake! Or else, when you shepherded my lambs in the field, I wish that some ravenous wolf had eaten you! Do you deny that I am your father, cursed slut?"

"Oh, burn her, burn her! Hanging is too good for her."

Hanging is a quicker and less painful way of dying than being burned at the stake.

The shepherd exited.

The Duke of York said, "Take her away, for she has lived too long and used that time to fill the world with vicious qualities."

Joan la Pucelle said, "First, let me tell you whom you have condemned to die. I am not one begotten by a shepherd peasant; instead, I issued from the progeny of Kings. I am virtuous and holy, chosen from above, by inspiration of celestial grace, to do work exceedingly exceptional on Earth. I never had to do with wicked spirits."

The word "do" has a sexual meaning. The sentence also meant this: "I never had anything to do with wicked spirits."

She continued, "But you, who are polluted with your lusts, who are stained with the guiltless blood of innocents, who are corrupt and tainted with a thousand vices, because you want the grace that others have, you judge it straightaway a thing impossible to accomplish wonders except by the help of devils.

"No, misconceived!"

By "misconceived," Joan la Pucelle may have meant that the Duke of York was wrong, or that he was illegitimate, or both.

She continued, "Joan of Arc has been a virgin from her tender infancy, chaste and immaculate in every thought, and her blood, thus cruelly spilled, will cry out for vengeance at the gates of Heaven."

"Yes, yes," the Duke of York said, impatiently. "Take her away to be executed!"

The Earl of Warwick said to the men who would burn her at the stake, "Listen, sirs, because she is a maiden, use plenty of wood; let there be enough to burn quickly and hotly. Place barrels of pitch leaning on the fatal stake, so that the torture of her death may be shortened."

The barrels of pitch would produce a thick smoke, suffocating Joan and killing her. This was a quicker and less painful death than dying from being burned.

"Will nothing change your unrelenting hearts?" Joan la Pucelle said. "Then, Joan, reveal your infirmity that law assures will give you the privilege of not yet being killed. I am with child, you bloodthirsty murderers. I am pregnant. Don't murder the fruit within my womb, although you eventually drag me to a violent death."

The Duke of York said, "Now Heaven forbid! The holy maiden is with child! This virgin is pregnant!"

The Earl of Warwick said to Joan, "This is the greatest miracle that you ever wrought. Has all your strict morality come to this?"

"She and the Dauphin have been juggling," the Duke of York said. "I wondered what would be her last defense, her last attempt to escape death."

"Juggling" meant "playing tricks." In this context, it also had a sexual meaning.

The Earl of Warwick said, "Bah, we'll allow no bastards to live, especially since Charles must be the father of it."

Joan la Pucelle said, "You are deceived; my child is not his. It was the Duke of Alençon who enjoyed my love."

"The Duke of Alençon!" the Duke of York said. "That notorious Machiavel!"

A Machiavel is a schemer. The word comes from Niccolo Machiavelli, author of *The Prince*, a pragmatic book that acknowledges that many Princes use immoral means to achieve their purposes.

The Duke of York added, "The bastard dies, and it would die even if it had a thousand lives."

"Oh, pardon me!" Joan la Pucelle said. "I have deceived and deluded you: It was neither Charles nor the Duke I named. Instead, it was Reignier, King of Naples, who prevailed."

"A married man!" the Earl of Warwick said. "That's most intolerable."

"Why, what a girl is here!" the Duke of York said. "I think she doesn't know well whom she may accuse of making her pregnant because she has had sex with so many men."

The Earl of Warwick said, "It's a sign she has been promiscuous and free."

"And yet, truly, she is a 'pure virgin,'" the Duke of York said sarcastically, adding, "Strumpet, your words condemn your brat and you. Don't beg for mercy, for it is in vain."

"Then lead me away," Joan la Pucelle said. "With all of you I leave my curse. May the glorious Sun never cast its beams upon the country — England — where you make your abode; instead, may darkness and the gloomy shade of death surround you, until catastrophe and despair drive you to break your necks or hang yourselves!"

The Duke of York said to her as the guards took her away, "May you break into pieces and be consumed by fire until you are ashes, you foul accursed minister of Hell!"

The Cardinal of Winchester arrived; with him were some attendants.

He said to the Duke of York, "Lord Regent, I greet your excellence with letters of commission from the King. For you should know, my lords, that the rulers of Christendom, moved with regret and sorrow for these outrageous, violent battles, have earnestly implored that a general peace be made between our nation of England and the aspiring French, and here at hand the Dauphin and his retinue are approaching in order to confer about some business."

"Is all our travail turned to this effect?" the Duke of York said. "Is this the result of all our effort and trouble? After the slaughter of so many peers, and so many Captains, gentlemen, and soldiers who in this quarrel have been overthrown and sold their bodies for their country's benefit, shall we at last conclude with an effeminate, unmanly peace? Haven't we lost because of treason, falsehood, and treachery the greater part of all the towns that our great progenitors such as King Henry V had conquered?

"Oh, Warwick, Earl of Warwick! I foresee with grief the utter loss of all the realm of France."

"Be patient, Duke of York," the Earl of Warwick said. "If we arrange a peace treaty with France, it shall be with such strict and severe conditions that the Frenchmen shall gain little thereby."

Charles the Dauphin, the Duke of Alençon, the Bastard of Orleans, Reignier, and others arrived.

Charles the Dauphin said, "Since, lords of England, it is thus agreed that a peaceful truce shall be proclaimed in France, we have come to be informed by you what the conditions of that peace treaty must be."

The Duke of York said, "Speak, Cardinal of Winchester; for boiling anger chokes the hollow passage of my poisoned voice because I see these our mortal enemies."

The Cardinal of Winchester said, "Charles, and the rest, this is what has been decreed. King Henry VI gives his consent, in pure compassion and mercifulness to ease your country of distressful war and allow you to breathe in fruitful peace, as long as you shall become true and loyal liegemen to his crown — and Charles, upon the condition you will swear to pay him tribute and be submissive to him, you shall be placed as Viceroy under him and you will continue to enjoy your regal dignity."

A Viceroy rules a country on behalf of another ruler to whom the Viceroy is subordinate.

The Duke of Alençon said, "Must he be then simply a shadow of himself? He will adorn his temples with a coronet, and yet, in substance and authority, retain only the privilege of a private man? This offer is absurd and reasonless."

Nobles, but not Kings, wore coronets. Kings wore crowns.

King Charles VI died two months after King Henry V of England had died. Now the citizens of France regarded Charles the Dauphin as King Charles VII of France. The English believed that King Henry VI of England was also the King of France.

Charles the Dauphin said, "It is known already that I possess more than half the Gallian — French — territories, and in those territories I am shown reverence as their lawful King. Shall I, for the gain of the territories I have not yet vanquished, take away so much from that prerogative of being acknowledged as King as to be called only the Viceroy of the whole?

"No, lord ambassador, I'd rather keep that which I have than, coveting more, be excluded from the possibility of being King of all France."

"Insulting Charles!" the Duke of York said. "Have you by secret means used intercession to obtain a league and a treaty, and now the matter draws toward a settlement, you stand aloof and quibble?

"Either accept the title you are usurping, which is a gift that comes from our King and is not anything you deserve, or we will plague you with incessant wars."

Reignier said quietly to Charles the Dauphin so that the English could not hear, "My lord, you don't do well by being obstinate and disputing details in the course of making this peace treaty. If once it is neglected, ten to one we shall not find the like opportunity to make another such treaty."

The Duke of Alençon said quietly to Charles the Dauphin so that the English could not hear, "To say the truth, it is your policy to save your subjects from such massacres and ruthless slaughters as are daily seen by our proceeding in hostility. Therefore make this peace treaty now, although you can break it later when you want to."

The Earl of Warwick asked, "What do you say, Charles? Shall our peace treaty stand?"

"It shall," Charles said, "with this condition. You will claim no interest in any of our French towns that are fortified with garrisons."

The Duke of York said, "Then swear allegiance to his majesty, King Henry VI, as you are a knight, never to disobey nor be rebellious to the crown of England. You and your nobles will swear never to disobey or be rebellious to the crown of England."

The Frenchmen knelt and swore.

The Duke of York said, "So, now dismiss your army when you please. Hang up your battle flags and let your drums be still and quiet, for here we enter upon a solemn peace."

In the royal palace in London, King Henry VI, the Earl of Suffolk, the Duke of Gloucester, and the Duke of Exeter met. Some attendants were present.

King Henry VI said to the Earl of Suffolk, "Your wondrous and splendid description, noble Earl, of beauteous Margaret has astonished me and filled me with wonder. Her virtues graced with external gifts breed love's deeply rooted passions in my heart, and just as the strength of tempestuous gusts of wind impels the mightiest ship against the tide, so I am driven by the report of her renown either to suffer shipwreck or arrive where I may have fruition of her love."

The Earl of Suffolk said, "Tush, my good lord, this superficial tale of her good qualities merely mentions those good qualities that are most apparent. It is only a preface of the praise that she deserves. The chief perfections of that lovely dame, had I sufficient skill to utter them, would make a whole book of enticing lines of praise that would be able to ravish and entrance any dull imagination, and which is more, she is not so divine, so fully replete with all choice delights, that she lacks humbleness of mind. She is content to be at your command. By command, I mean the command of virtuous and chaste intentions, to love and honor you, Henry VI, as her lord and husband."

King Henry VI said, "And otherwise I, Henry, will never presume. My intentions toward her are honorable.

"Therefore, my Lord Protector, give consent that Margaret may become England's royal Queen."

The Duke of Gloucester replied, "If I would give consent to that, I would be giving consent to glossing over and extenuating sin. You know, my lord, that your highness is betrothed to another lady of esteem: You are engaged to marry the daughter of the Earl of Armagnac. How shall we then dispense with that contract of marriage, and not disfigure your honor with reproach?"

The Earl of Suffolk said, "As does a ruler with unlawful oaths."

King Henry VI's oath, however, to marry the daughter of the Earl of Armagnac was not unlawful.

The Earl of Suffolk continued, "Or as does one who, at a tournament having vowed to test his strength, yet does not engage in a joust because of his adversary's odds. A poor Earl's daughter is unequal odds, and therefore the marriage contract may be broken without offence."

Dukes outranked Earls, and Kings outranked Dukes. The Earl of Suffolk was saying that a King could do much better than to marry the daughter of an Earl.

The Duke of Gloucester asked, "Why, what, I earnestly ask, is Margaret more than that? Her father is no better than an Earl, although he excels in glorious titles."

He meant that some of the glorious titles were titular, in name only; for example, they brought no money to Margaret's father, who was poor for a person of his rank.

"Yes, lord, her father is better than an Earl. He is a King, the King of Naples and Jerusalem, and he has such great authority in France that this alliance — our King married to his daughter — will confirm our peace and keep the Frenchmen in allegiance."

The Duke of Gloucester objected, "And so the Earl of Armagnac may do because he is a close relative of Charles the Dauphin."

"Besides," the Duke of Exeter said, "the wealth of the Earl of Armagnac guarantees a liberal and generous dowry, where Reignier will sooner receive than give. Reignier is poor."

"A dowry, my lords!" the Earl of Suffolk said. "Don't disgrace your King like this. Don't say that he is so abject, base, and poor that he must choose a wife on the basis of wealth and not on that of perfect love. Henry is able to enrich his Queen and does not need to seek a Queen who will make him rich. That is the way worthless peasants bargain for their wives; they are market men who buy and sell oxen, sheep, and horses. Marriage is a matter of more worth than to be dealt in by attorneys and the drawing up of contracts.

"Not whom we want, but whom his grace the King wants, must be the companion of his nuptial bed. And therefore, lords, since he loves her most, this is the reason that must be most binding on us out of all these reasons, and so in our opinions Margaret should be preferred as King Henry VI's wife.

"For what is forced wedlock but a Hell, a lifetime of discord and continual strife? In contrast, the contrary — a marriage that is chosen, not forced — brings bliss, and is a pattern of celestial, Heavenly peace.

"Whom should we match with Henry, who is a King, but Margaret, who is daughter to a King? Her peerless features, joined with her noble birth, proves her fit for none but a King.

"Her valiant courage and undaunted spirit, more than is commonly seen in women, will give us what we hope for in the children of a King because Henry VI, the son of a conqueror, is likely to beget more conquerors, if he is linked in love with a lady of as high resolve as is fair Margaret.

"So then yield, my lords; and here conclude with me that Margaret shall be Queen of England, and none but she."

King Henry VI said, "Whether it be through the forcefulness of your report of her, my noble Lord of Suffolk, or because my tender youth was never yet touched with any passion of inflaming love, I cannot tell, but of this I am assured, I feel such sharp dissension in my breast, such fierce alarums both of hope and fear, that the working of my thoughts is making me sick.

"Take, therefore, a voyage on a ship; hurry, my lord, to France. Agree to any legal contracts, and take measures to ensure that Lady Margaret will agree to cross the seas to England and be crowned King Henry VI's faithful and anointed Queen.

"For your expenses and sufficient outlay of money, from among the people gather up a tenth of their income as a tax."

English citizens hated such taxes.

King Henry VI continued, "Be gone, I say, for until you return I remain bewildered with a thousand worries.

"And you, good uncle of Gloucester, take no offence at my decision to marry Margaret. If you judge me by what you were when you were younger, not by what you are now, I know it will excuse this swift execution of my will."

The Duke of Gloucester's first "marriage" was controversial and illegal. He "married" the Lady Jaquet, the legal wife of John, Duke of Brabant.

King Henry VI continued, "And so conduct me where, away from company, alone, I may consider and meditate on my grief."

His grief was his not being with Margaret.

King Henry VI and his attendants exited.

The Duke of Gloucester said, "Yes, grief, I am afraid, both at first and last, both at the beginning and the end."

This kind of grief was trouble. He believed that King Henry VI's marrying Margaret would bring bitter trouble to England.

The Duke of Gloucester and the Duke of Exeter exited.

Alone, the Earl of Suffolk said to himself, "Thus I, Suffolk, have prevailed; and thus I go, as the youthful Paris went once to Greece, with hope to find the like event in love, but prosper better than the Trojan did."

The Trojan Prince Paris caused the Trojan War by going to Sparta, Greece, and running off with Helen, the wife of Menelaus, the King of Sparta.

The Earl of Suffolk was saying that he hoped to sleep with Margaret, but that he hoped to do so without having to suffer such bad consequences as a war.

He continued, "Margaret shall now be Queen of England, and rule the King. But I will rule her, the King, and the realm of England."

Appendix A: Brief Historical Background

KING EDWARD I: 1272-1307

Edward Longshanks fought and defeated the Welsh chieftains, and he made his eldest son the Prince of Wales. He won victories against the Scots, and he brought the coronation stone from Scone to Westminster.

KING EDWARD II: 1307-deposed 1327

At the Battle of Bannockburn in 1314, the Scots defeated his army. His wife and her lover, Mortimer, deposed him. According to legend, he was murdered in Berkeley Castle by means of a red-hot poker thrust up his anus.

KING EDWARD III: 1327-1377

Son of King Edward II, he reigned for a long time — 50 years. Because he wanted to conquer Scotland and France, he started the Hundred Years War in 1338. King Edward III and his eldest son, Edward the Black Prince, won important victories against the French in the Battle of Crécy (1346) and the Battle of Poitiers (1356).

One of King Edward III's sons was John of Gaunt, first Duke of Lancaster.

Another of King Edward III's sons was Edmund of Langley, first Duke of York.

During his reign, the Black Death — the bubonic plague — struck in 1348-1350 and killed half of England's population.

KING RICHARD II: 1377-deposed 1399

King Richard II was the son of Edward the Black Prince. In 1381, Wat Tyler led the Peasants Revolt, which was suppressed. King Richard II sent Henry, Duke of Lancaster, into exile and seized Henry's estates, but in 1399 Henry, Duke of Lancaster, returned from exile and deposed King Richard II, thereby becoming King Henry IV. In 1400, King Richard II was murdered in Pontefract Castle, which is also known as Pomfret Castle.

HOUSE OF LANCASTER

KING HENRY IV: 1399-1413

Henry, Duke of Lancaster, was the son of John of Gaunt, who was the third son of King Edward III. He was born at Bolingbroke Castle and so was also known as Henry of Bolingbroke. Returning from exile in France to reclaim his estates, he deposed King Richard II. He spent the 13 years of his reign putting down rebellions and defending himself against those who would assassinate or depose him. The Welshman Owen Glendower and the English Percy family were among those who fought against him. King Henry IV died at the age of 45.

KING HENRY V: 1413-1422

The son of King Henry IV, King Henry V renewed the war with France. He and his army defeated the French at the Battle of Agincourt (1415) despite being heavily outnumbered. He married Catherine of Valoise, the daughter of the French King, but he died before becoming King of France. He left behind a 10-month-old son, who became King Henry VI.

KING HENRY VI: 1422-deposed 1461; briefly returned to the throne in 1470-1471

The Hundred Years War ended in 1453; the English lost all land in France except for Calais, a port city. After King Henry VI suffered an attack of mental illness in 1454, Richard, third Duke of York and the father of King Henry IV and King Richard III, was made Protector of the Realm. England suffered civil war after the House of York challenged King Henry VI's right to be King of England. In 1470, King Henry VI was briefly restored to the English throne. In 1471, he was murdered in the Tower of London. A short time previously, his son, Edward, Prince of Wales, had been killed at the Battle of Tewkesbury in 1471; this was the final battle in the Wars of the Roses. The Yorkists decisively defeated the Lancastrians.

King Henry VI founded both Eton College and King's College, Cambridge.

WARS OF THE ROSES

From 1455-1487, the Yorkists and the Lancastrians fought for power in England in the famous Wars of the Roses. The emblem of the York family was a white rose, and the emblem of the Lancaster family was a red rose. The Yorkists and the Lancastrians were descended from King Edward III.

HOUSE OF YORK

KING EDWARD IV: 1461-1483 (King Henry VI briefly returned to the throne in 1470-1471)

Son of Richard, third Duke of York, he charged his brother George, Duke of Clarence, with treason and had him murdered in 1478. After dying suddenly, he left behind two sons aged 12 and 9, and five daughters.

His surviving two brothers in Shakespeare's play *Richard III* are these: 1) George, Duke of Clarence. Clarence is the second-oldest brother; and 2) Richard, Duke of Gloucester, and afterwards King Richard III. Gloucester is the youngest surviving brother.

William Caxton established the first printing press in Westminster during King Edward IV's reign.

KING EDWARD V: 1483-1483

The eldest son of King Edward IV, he reigned for only two months, the shortest-lived monarch in English history. He was 13 years old. He and his younger brother, Richard, were murdered in the Tower of London. According to Shakespeare's play, their uncle, Richard, Duke of Gloucester, who became King Richard III, was responsible for their murders.

KING RICHARD III: 1483-1485

Brother of King Edward IV, Richard, the Duke of Gloucester, declared the two Princes in the Tower of London — King Edward V and Richard, Duke of York — illegitimate and made himself King Richard III. In 1485, Henry Tudor, Earl of Richmond, a descendant of John of Gaunt, who was the father of King Henry IV, defeated King Richard III at the Battle of Bosworth Field in Leicestershire. King Richard III died in that battle.

King Richard III's father was Richard Plantagenet, Duke of York. His mother was Cecily Neville, Duchess of York.

King Richard III's death in the Battle of Bosworth Field is regarded as marking the end of the Middle Ages in England.

A NOTE ON THE PLANTAGENETS

The first Plantagenet King was King Henry II (1154-1189). From 1154 until 1485, when King Richard III died, all English Kings were Plantagenets. Both the Lancaster family and the York family were Plantagenets.

Geoffrey Plantagenet, Count of Anjou, was the founder of the House of Plantagenet. Geoffrey's son, Henry Curtmantle, became King Henry II of England, thereby founding the Plantagenet dynasty. Geoffrey wore a sprig of broom, a flowering shrub, as a badge; the Latin name for broom is *planta genista*, and from it the name "Plantagenet" arose.

The Plantagenet dynasty can be divided into three parts:

1154-1216: The Angevins. The Angevin Kings were Henry II, Richard I (Richard the Lionheart), and John 1.

1216-1399: The Plantagenets. These Kings ranged from King Henry III to King Richard II.

1399-1485: The Houses of Lancaster and of York. These Kings ranged from King Henry IV to King Richard III.

BEGINNING OF THE TUDOR DYNASTY

KING HENRY VII: 1485-1509

When King Richard III fell at the Battle of Bosworth, Henry Tudor, Earl of Richmond, became King Henry VII. A Lancastrian, he married Elizabeth of York — young Elizabeth of York in *Richard III* — and united the two warring houses, York and Lancaster, thus ending the Wars of the Roses. One of his grandfathers was Sir Owen Tudor, who married Catherine of Valoise, widow of King Henry V.

KING HENRY VIII: 1509-1547

King Henry VIII had six wives. These are their fates: "Divorced, Beheaded, Died, Divorced, Beheaded, Survived." He divorced his first wife, Catherine of Aragon, so that he could marry Anne Boleyn. Because of this, England divorced itself from the Catholic Church, and King Henry VIII became the head of the Church of England. King Henry VIII had one son and two daughters, all of whom became rulers of England: Edward, daughter of Jane Seymour; Mary, daughter of Catherine of Aragon; and Elizabeth, daughter of Anne Boleyn.

KING EDWARD VI: 1547-1553

The son of Henry VIII and Jane Seymour, King Edward VI succeeded his father at the age of nine; a Council of Regency with his uncle, Duke of Somerset, styled Protector, ruled the government.

During King Edward VI's reign, Archbishop Thomas Cranmer wrote the 1549 Book of Common Prayer.

When King Edward VI died, Lady Jane Grey was proclaimed Queen, but she ruled for only nine days before being executed in 1554, aged 17. Mary, daughter of Catherine of Aragon, became Queen. She was Catholic, thus the attempt to make Lady Jane Grey, a Protestant, Queen.

QUEEN MARY I (BLOODY MARY) 1553-1558

Queen Mary I attempted to make England a Catholic nation again. Some Protestant bishops, including Archbishop Thomas Cranmer, were burnt at the stake, and other violence broke out, resulting in her being known as Bloody Mary.

QUEEN ELIZABETH I: 1558-1603

The daughter of King Henry VIII and Anne Boleyn, Queen Elizabeth I was a popular Queen. In 1588, the English navy decisively defeated the Spanish Armada. England had many notable playwrights and poets, including William Shakespeare and Ben Jonson, during her reign. She never married and had no children.

KING JAMES I OF ENGLAND: A MEMBER OF THE HOUSE OF STUART

KING JAMES I OF ENGLAND AND VI OF SCOTLAND: 1603-1625

King James I of England was the son of Mary, Queen of Scots, and Lord Darnley. In 1605 Guy Fawkes and his Catholic co-conspirators were captured before they could blow up the Houses of Parliament; this was known as the Gunpowder Plot.

In 1611, during King James I's reign, the Authorized Version of the Bible (the King James Version) was completed.

Also during King James I's reign, in 1620 the Pilgrims sailed for America in their ship *The Mayflower*.

A NOTE ON SHAKESPEARE

William Shakespeare lived under two monarchs: Queen Elizabeth I and King James I.

Appendix B: About the Author

It was a dark and stormy night. Suddenly a cry rang out, and on a hot summer night in 1954, Josephine, wife of Carl Bruce, gave birth to a boy — me. Unfortunately, this young married couple allowed Reuben Saturday, Josephine's brother, to name their first-born. Reuben, aka "The Joker," decided that Bruce was a nice name, so he decided to name me Bruce Bruce. I have gone by my middle name — David — ever since.

Being named Bruce David Bruce hasn't been all bad. Bank tellers remember me very quickly, so I don't often have to show an ID. It can be fun in charades, also. When I was a counselor as a teenager at Camp Echoing Hills in Warsaw, Ohio, a fellow counselor gave the signs for "sounds like" and "two words," then she pointed to a bruise on her leg twice. Bruise Bruise? Oh yeah, Bruce Bruce is the answer!

Uncle Reuben, by the way, gave me a haircut when I was in kindergarten. He cut my hair short and shaved a small bald spot on the back of my head. My mother wouldn't let me go to school until the bald spot grew out again.

Of all my brothers and sisters (six in all), I am the only transplant to Athens, Ohio. I was born in Newark, Ohio, and have lived all around Southeastern Ohio. However, I moved to Athens to go to Ohio University and have never left.

At Ohio U, I never could make up my mind whether to major in English or Philosophy, so I got a bachelor's degree with a double major in both areas, then I added a master's degree in English and a master's degree in Philosophy.

Currently, and for a long time to come (I eat fruits and veggies), I am spending my retirement writing books such as *Nadia Comaneci: Perfect 10*, *The Funniest People in Dance*, *Homer's* Iliad: *A Retelling in Prose*, and *William Shakespeare's* Othello: *A Retelling in Prose*.

By the way, my sister Brenda Kennedy writes romances such as *A New Beginning* and *Shattered Dreams*.

Appendix C: Some Books by David Bruce

Retellings of a Classic Work of Literature

Arden of Faversham: *A Retelling*

Ben Jonson's The Alchemist: *A Retelling*

Ben Jonson's The Arraignment, or Poetaster: *A Retelling*

Ben Jonson's Bartholomew Fair: *A Retelling*

Ben Jonson's The Case is Altered: *A Retelling*

Ben Jonson's Catiline's Conspiracy: *A Retelling*

Ben Jonson's The Devil is an Ass: *A Retelling*

Ben Jonson's Epicene: *A Retelling*

Ben Jonson's Every Man in His Humor: *A Retelling*

Ben Jonson's Every Man Out of His Humor: *A Retelling*

Ben Jonson's The Fountain of Self-Love, or Cynthia's Revels: *A Retelling*

Ben Jonson's The Magnetic Lady, or Humors Reconciled: *A Retelling*

Ben Jonson's The New Inn, or The Light Heart: *A Retelling*

Ben Jonson's Sejanus' Fall: *A Retelling*

Ben Jonson's The Staple of News: *A Retelling*

Ben Jonson's A Tale of a Tub: *A Retelling*

Ben Jonson's Volpone, or the Fox: *A Retelling*

Christopher Marlowe's Complete Plays: Retellings

Christopher Marlowe's Dido, Queen of Carthage: *A Retelling*

Christopher Marlowe's Doctor Faustus: *Retellings of the 1604 A-Text and of the 1616 B-Text*

Christopher Marlowe's Edward II: *A Retelling*

Christopher Marlowe's The Massacre at Paris: *A Retelling*

Christopher Marlowe's The Rich Jew of Malta: *A Retelling*

Christopher Marlowe's Tamburlaine, Parts 1 and 2: *Retellings*

Dante's Divine Comedy: *A Retelling in Prose*

Dante's Inferno: *A Retelling in Prose*

Dante's Purgatory: *A Retelling in Prose*

Dante's Paradise: *A Retelling in Prose*

The Famous Victories of Henry V: *A Retelling*

From the Iliad *to the* Odyssey: *A Retelling in Prose of Quintus of Smyrna's* Posthomerica

George Chapman, Ben Jonson, and John Marston's Eastward Ho! *A Retelling*

George Peele's The Arraignment of Paris: *A Retelling*

George Peele's The Battle of Alcazar: *A Retelling*

George Peele's David and Bathsheba, and the Tragedy of Absalom: *A Retelling*

George Peele's Edward I: *A Retelling*

George Peele's The Old Wives' Tale: *A Retelling*

George-a-Greene: *A Retelling*

The History of King Leir: *A Retelling*

Homer's Iliad: *A Retelling in Prose*

Homer's Odyssey: *A Retelling in Prose*

J.W. Gent.'s The Valiant Scot: A Retelling

Jason and the Argonauts: A Retelling in Prose of Apollonius of Rhodes' Argonautica

John Ford: Eight Plays Translated into Modern English

John Ford's The Broken Heart: *A Retelling*

John Ford's The Fancies, Chaste and Noble: *A Retelling*

John Ford's The Lady's Trial: *A Retelling*

John Ford's The Lover's Melancholy: *A Retelling*

John Ford's Love's Sacrifice: *A Retelling*

John Ford's Perkin Warbeck: *A Retelling*

John Ford's The Queen: *A Retelling*

John Ford's 'Tis Pity She's a Whore: *A Retelling*

John Lyly's Campaspe: *A Retelling*

John Lyly's Endymion, The Man in the Moon: *A Retelling*

John Lyly's Galatea: *A Retelling*

John Lyly's Love's Metamorphosis: *A Retelling*

John Lyly's Midas: *A Retelling*

John Lyly's Mother Bombie: *A Retelling*

John Lyly's Sappho and Phao: *A Retelling*

John Lyly's The Woman in the Moon: *A Retelling*

John Webster's The White Devil: *A Retelling*

King Edward III: *A Retelling*

Mankind: *A Medieval Morality Play* (A Retelling)

Margaret Cavendish's The Unnatural Tragedy: *A Retelling*

The Merry Devil of Edmonton: *A Retelling*

The Summoning of Everyman: *A Medieval Morality Play* (A Retelling)

Robert Greene's Friar Bacon and Friar Bungay: *A Retelling*

The Taming of a Shrew: *A Retelling*

Tarlton's Jests: A Retelling

Thomas Middleton's A Chaste Maid in Cheapside: *A Retelling*

Thomas Middleton's Women Beware Women: *A Retelling*

Thomas Middleton and Thomas Dekker's The Roaring Girl: *A Retelling*

Thomas Middleton and William Rowley's The Changeling: *A Retelling*

The Trojan War and Its Aftermath: Four Ancient Epic Poems

Virgil's Aeneid: *A Retelling in Prose*

William Shakespeare's 5 Late Romances: Retellings in Prose

William Shakespeare's 10 Histories: Retellings in Prose

William Shakespeare's 11 Tragedies: Retellings in Prose

William Shakespeare's 12 Comedies: Retellings in Prose

William Shakespeare's 38 Plays: Retellings in Prose

William Shakespeare's 1 Henry IV, aka Henry IV, Part 1: *A Retelling in Prose*

William Shakespeare's 2 Henry IV, aka Henry IV, Part 2: *A Retelling in Prose*

William Shakespeare's 1 Henry VI, aka Henry VI, Part 1: *A Retelling in Prose*

William Shakespeare's 2 Henry VI, aka Henry VI, Part 2: *A Retelling in Prose*

William Shakespeare's 3 Henry VI, aka Henry VI, Part 3: *A Retelling in Prose*

William Shakespeare's All's Well that Ends Well: *A Retelling in Prose*

William Shakespeare's Antony and Cleopatra: *A Retelling in Prose*

William Shakespeare's As You Like It: *A Retelling in Prose*

William Shakespeare's The Comedy of Errors: *A Retelling in Prose*

William Shakespeare's Coriolanus: *A Retelling in Prose*

William Shakespeare's Cymbeline: *A Retelling in Prose*

William Shakespeare's Hamlet: *A Retelling in Prose*

William Shakespeare's Henry V: *A Retelling in Prose*

William Shakespeare's Henry VIII: *A Retelling in Prose*

William Shakespeare's Julius Caesar: *A Retelling in Prose*

William Shakespeare's King John: *A Retelling in Prose*

William Shakespeare's King Lear: *A Retelling in Prose*

William Shakespeare's Love's Labor's Lost: *A Retelling in Prose*

William Shakespeare's Macbeth: *A Retelling in Prose*

William Shakespeare's Measure for Measure: *A Retelling in Prose*

William Shakespeare's The Merchant of Venice: *A Retelling in Prose*

William Shakespeare's The Merry Wives of Windsor: *A Retelling in Prose*

William Shakespeare's A Midsummer Night's Dream: *A Retelling in Prose*

William Shakespeare's Much Ado About Nothing: *A Retelling in Prose*

William Shakespeare's Othello: *A Retelling in Prose*

William Shakespeare's Pericles, Prince of Tyre: *A Retelling in Prose*

William Shakespeare's Richard II: *A Retelling in Prose*

William Shakespeare's Richard III: *A Retelling in Prose*

William Shakespeare's Romeo and Juliet: *A Retelling in Prose*

William Shakespeare's The Taming of the Shrew: *A Retelling in Prose*

William Shakespeare's The Tempest: *A Retelling in Prose*

William Shakespeare's Timon of Athens: *A Retelling in Prose*

William Shakespeare's Titus Andronicus: *A Retelling in Prose*

William Shakespeare's Troilus and Cressida: *A Retelling in Prose*

William Shakespeare's Twelfth Night: *A Retelling in Prose*

William Shakespeare's The Two Gentlemen of Verona: *A Retelling in Prose*

William Shakespeare's The Two Noble Kinsmen: *A Retelling in Prose*

William Shakespeare's The Winter's Tale: *A Retelling in Prose*